Into the Presence

Harold A. Lawrence

All rights reserved. No part of this book may be reprinted, stored in a retrieval system, transmitted electronically or otherwise, without the written permission of the publisher.

ISBN: 1-890307-07-6

Copyright © 1998

Boyd Publishing Company
PO Box 367
Milledgeville, Georgia 31061

To My Parents
Harold & Ruby Lawrence

Acknowledgement

Gratitude is expressed to Wilbur and Lucy Baugh whose generosity made the printing of this book possible.

Foreword

The three point sermon, while considered by many to be of antiquated style, has been a useful preaching tool in my ministry. While these sermons reflect that style, they are not critically dependent upon it. I am deeply grateful to my manuscript readers, twenty in all, who gave me many insights and taught me a number of valuable things; chiefly, that the spoken word is not the same when committed to print.

Many preachers do well as speakers and not so well as writers. One reason for this is that the persona of the speaker often does not translate to the printed page. Therefore, it is incumbent upon the preacher as writer to dispense with euphemisms and cliches to the degree that the written word can transcend the spoken word.

The challenge of preaching is to find fresh ways to say and communicate much which is old and understood. That is never an easy task. Harder still is the conversion from one medium to another without losing the integrity of a sermon in the process. It is a delicate wire on which to walk, and friends rarely love us enough to tell us when we have fallen off.

If these sermons can stimulate a curiosity about scripture passages and a renewed sense of inquiry for lay readers, then they will have been worth the effort made to adapt them to the printed page. Finding a new and cutting edge for one's perceptions and thoughts, discovering a shard or two of theological excitement in the field of the ordinary is a reasonable expectation when one commits time and attention to reading material of this nature. In that spirit, these sermons are offered as devices to stretch the faith horizon.

It is my hope that this series will challenge those who preach to contemplate the "inner journey" for themselves and to develop their own fresh perspectives of what God is like and what it means to belong in God's presence. After all, if those of us who preach assume that we are taking people anywhere, this is generally the direction we allude to and affirm. Also needing affirmation are the provocative questions: How do I understand my experience of God? Do I have an accurate understanding? How do I act upon it and where is it taking me? It is the task of the preacher to connect people with these questions and to accompany them spiritually, intellectually and emotionally as they seek the answers.

-Harold Lawrence

About the Author

Harold Lawrence graduated from Wofford College, received his M.Div. and D.Min. degrees from Emory University. He has been a United Methodist pastor for thirty years and is the author of numerous historical and poetical works. *Into the Presence* was compiled during his tenure at the First United Methodist Church, Milledgeville, Georgia.

Introduction

An elderly relative of mine told me about his conversion. Reared in a deeply religious family, he was troubled because he could not grasp the Christian faith for himself. When the pastor visited to counsel with him, a remarkable thing occurred. "All he did was walk in the room and instantly it all came clear to me." He wondered at the gift of that day.

In his sermons, *Into the Presence*, Dr. Harold Lawrence is telling us that in addition to being a wondrous, once-for-all gift, faith is also a journey, a process. Faith has a giveness, a conviction and a surety in it; but faith also unfolds, and develops, and grows throughout one's whole life, bringing renewal and new understanding. Lawrence devotes his book to reminding us, in many different ways, that being a follower of Christ means just that — following Christ on a journey of life with its demands, its rewards, its surprises. There is no comfortable Christian.

In intriguing ways, this series plays upon the journeying theme. Like some of the mystical Christians of our Western middle ages — John of the Cross comes to mind — Lawrence challenges us to detach from the familiar, from the routine and conventional (especially in religion) and prepare ourselves for serious questions, for new discoveries, for movement forward. His own personal experience richly details some of the pieces: a family in a mobile home, or three young Harikrishnas who seek refuge in a downpour. Lawrence is an early morning jogger, and many insights from that "journey" appear. Again, he cites Jesus' disciples when the realization dawns on them that they must not only tell Jesus' teachings to others, they must illustrate them in their lives as they go. The sermon on death as journey opens a horizon that will almost certainly bring responses and questions.

An element of mystery in these pieces may well lead readers/hearers to say, "What journey? Where do you and Jesus want us to go?" As if by design Lawrence lets the theme of journey build and build throughout the early selections, while keeping a certain suspense. "Show us this journey!" By hints and instances we begin to realize what he means, in part, the journey to the human being near at hand, someone in need, someone overlooked, someone who needs our going the extra mile. He means a journey to other human beings as they really are, if we take time to realize and see. But there is more: He means things close to ourselves about God and the world that we did not recognize. He calls them, in a fine phrase, "the unclaimed possessions of the heart."

Pascal said, "God is in the seeking for him." Lawrence warns us not to be deceived by the things we rush to seize upon, as if they were God. Don't forget the journey. St. Augustine describes the original sin of the Garden as a monumental shortcut. The serpent's temptation of Adam and Eve, "You will be like gods," was true! The Creator wanted them to be like God — in love, kindness, justice, goodness. Their sin was in rushing to seize that status without going the journey: Have it now! On your own terms. St. Augustine said they could have become Godlike had they been obedient to God's long way. Harold Lawrence tells us that we dare not miss the journey.

William Mallard
Emory University
June, 1998

GETTING IN STEP
Luke 16:16

"The law and the prophets were until John; since then the good news of the kingdom of God is preached, and every one enters it violently." (Luke 16:16)

A group of young boys led by two older ones went for a Saturday hike. Looking forward to an adventurous day together, they came to a stream almost out of its banks and swollen from recent rains. They found a place to cross where two floating logs bridged the current, and it was decided that they would go one at a time. Who would go first? One of the younger boys, eager to display his courage and enthusiasm, volunteered to show the rest how to do it. He started out, one foot on each log. In mid-stream, the logs separated slightly because of his movement. Noticing this, he stopped. And ever so slowly, the logs began to drift away from each other. His companions on the bank saw his stance grow wider and wider, leaving him with no leverage to jump to either log. As they watched, the youngster lost his balance and toppled into the water.

What a fitting picture for today's follower of Christ! One foot in the world and the other in God's kingdom, unable to find a firm footing in either! Jesus told one person who had a mental grasp of what He was saying, "You are not far from the Kingdom of God!" (Mark 12:34). But what would He say to believers today? More likely than not, He would point out the fact that they are in danger of completely missing the Kingdom.

Today's Christians almost always have an identity problem. They identify themselves as Christ's people on Sunday, and they are taught and preached to about the values of His Kingdom. Then they go back home and identify themselves with the world, and they practice the values of the kingdom of this world. It has become such a customary practice for so long that not the slightest attention is paid to the existence of a double-standard. No one seems concerned about straddling these particular logs. Everyone has adjusted perfectly.

The Christ of our spiritual road reminds us that we cannot have it both ways. Yes, one may practice religion and then go where one chooses, but one cannot be in step with Christ and, at the same time, walk a different road. There is a profound difference between religion and spirituality. Religion is what one thinks it is, believes it to be, decides to accept and practice! Spirituality is what one touches beyond opinions and beliefs when one's spirit is available and open to God.

A friend of mine tells me that two of the great forces at work in human interaction are agenda and process. Being a therapist, he is more inclined toward trusting process than toward adopting agenda. An agenda is usually something intended and imposed in order to gain a solution. Process, on the other hand, is something awaited and observed and accepted in order to gain a solution. These two great dynamics are very much a part of our faith tradition. The history of the church is filled with agenda and, at the same time, is brimming with process. They both have their good groundings in Paul, the master of agenda, and in Jesus, the convener of process. The astounding consequence of faith in our time is that while process has been entrusted to the Holy Spirit, agenda has been entrusted to human beings.

Go down the average pew on a given Sunday. The agendas would amaze you. If you could ask each person, "What are you doing here?" and be told the truth, these are some of the answers you would be likely to hear: "I am hedging my bets in case there is a God and a life beyond this one. I just haven't told anybody!" or "I'm here to come to know and influence a visible portion of the community, establishing my image so no one will forget it. I just haven't told anybody!" or "I enjoy the comfort and the safety of belonging here. It meets my needs, and I get what I want from it. I just haven't told anybody!"

The agendas are incredible, but guess what! Christ knows them all! Men and women who think of themselves as Christians can adopt all the agendas they please. But deep down in the pit of who they are, they know that they are disconnected from the process, and they are out of step with the Christ who would have them join Him on the road.

There is a church where another friend of mine is pastor. He tells me that one cannot become a member of that church unless he or she goes through eight weeks of preparation and training for membership, even when coming from other United Methodist churches. One person who wanted to join remarked that, "I've been a Methodist all my life. I don't need to go to this class." And the response was, "You have been a Methodist all your life, but have you been a Christian?"

There are so many agendas which have come with church membership and which have given many this double identity by which they try to walk in the world while keeping one foot in God's kingdom. This is the predicament of Christianity in our time; this is why it is changing little rather than much; this is why it is winning fewer amd fewer rather than more and more. There is an identity problem in the Christian Church, and until it is resolved, people will not do anything about the Kingdom of God but meander around in the idea of it one morning a week.

Coming to ultimate terms with the truth about one's life and being may not be on anyone's itinerary, but Christ demands this kind of prerequisite to one's faith. His gospel is disturbing. It arouses people out of their comfort and their security. It disturbs their agendas, and it would destroy them before their eyes.

In one of His statements about the Kingdom, Jesus said, "every one enters it violently." He created a mental picture of those who had been prevented entry due to the limits of the Law suddenly becoming aggressive about being included. Such was their excitement that they would push and force their way into the Kingdom, claiming it for themselves as they would claim anything else. Jesus cautioned them, however, that the Kingdom could not be gained solely by their initiative. To find the Kingdom, to have it, to possess its riches required more than the desire to seize it as one would a prize. Its great pre-requisite was the destruction of self-fulfilling agendas, even the one that would have the Kingdom for oneself.

Everybody wants to be happy. Everybody wants to enjoy the love of God. Everybody wants to belong in God's Kingdom. Everyone has a spiritual agenda, yet when Christ speaks about the Kingdom, He is talking about process. To those who would force their way into it, He would show that any steps taken in its direction seem always to move one backward. And it is in this great collision of one's agenda with God's process that the Christ of the road is discovered.

The time inevitably comes to get in step with the one who points unmistakably at our spirit and says, "Follow!" Those of us who have been afraid to admit where we've been and where we are going, who just plod ahead wearing spiritual blinders which limit our knowing or owning the truth about ourselves must wake up to what life is really like without Him and begin to trust this process. And when we do, the first step we will take on this inward journey will be one that feels like two steps backward. It is called **contrition**. Contrition, that sincere remorse one feels for how one has lived, is the first violent shock that we give to our heart of hearts as we move from the kingdom of the world to the one that Christ commends.

It was at the close of the evening service. The visiting preacher had spoken about the importance of giving one's life to God. He gave a moving invitation for people to pray at the altar as the lights were dimmed and the piano played softly. Nobody came forward to pray, not even the church's preacher who customarily did on such occasions. The visiting preacher just stood there in the pulpit, gripping the sides of it. After a few moments, he came down and prayed alone. It wasn't one of those polite gestures done to close things out. It was a laboring prayer. Those watching him from the back could sense his struggle. When he got up to return to the chancel area, his face was wet and his eyes were red. A common thought ran through the people like a current. "What in the world has he done to warrant a prayer like that?" And then it began to register with all of them. Aside from wrestling with his own issues, he was serving as a model for those who did not come.

Into every quiet and controlled faith agenda, even the eager and impetuous ones, comes this process which causes the human heart to take stock, regroup, reconsider, realign. In the moment when one feels that false sense of security about her relationship with God; at the height of one's experiencing that false sense of justification in his Christian lifestyle; right in midstride while taking all of the practiced steps, comes this lightning insight about who one really is and where one really is among all of the religious gymnastics and routines that have insulated the spirit from God's will and God's way. Crashing into one's meditative moments comes God's great, unnerving moment. It is invitational, yet it almost always requires the abandonment of one's familiar and benign faith agendas.

In order to follow Christ, in order to embark on an inner journey which is authentic and spiritually reconstituting, one has to get in step with this process which would move us unerringly and deliberately in God's direction. First of all, there has to be contrition. Then there must be **confession.** Confession comes when that great statement surfaces in the mind and heart: "Father, forgive me, for I have sinned." Such an old and classic prayer needs to be repeated until it is believed and until liberation is found from it.

While filling out a self-evaluation form, a young pastor struggled with what to put down in the area set aside for needed personal improvements. He did not want to admit that he was inadequate in any area, especially on a form which would be read by his superintendent. He was frustrated over what to put down. It gnawed at him and worked on him until he became angry at having to contend with such a stupid form. Ever so gradually, he felt a sense of desperation build in him. It wasn't only because of the form. He began to open the spiritual door just a crack, and he felt a flood of doubt and fear come over him.

He closed his eyes and tried to pray. It was a jumble of cluttered words that were absolutely meaningless. Like wrestling with an angel, this young man struggled to find the right connecting link and could not find one. He even hashed through for himself that request the disciples made of Jesus, "Lord, teach me to pray," but nothing would work for him. It confirmed something he already knew. Nothing had worked for a long time. Finally, he opened his eyes and wrote on the form that he had a deficit in his prayer life. That deficit wasn't erased because he wrote it down. But by honestly confessing it, he made a small step forward. Thereafter, when he prayed, he began each time with the words, "Lord, be merciful to me, a sinner."

"If we confess our sins," says the scripture, "He is faithful and just and will forgive our sins and cleanse us from all unrighteousness." Where are we in this process which moves us in God's direction? Where are we when our self-fulfilling Christianity is so out of sync with Christ that we would pervert His words to fit our agendas? "Seek ye first the Kingdom of God," He said. But you and I have used Him and used God and used the Church to oil our hinges in the world. We have not humbled ourselves and confessed our sins because they seem like two steps backward rather than progressive steps.

For this great spiritual reckoning to happen in your life and mine, we must also dash pride and ego and conceit to pieces, and we must kneel in contrition and confession. If and when we do, we find that we are compelled to go a step further. We must **change.** We know the drill forward and backward. Sometimes called conversion, it is as old as our faith tradition. Repent! Turn around! Go in the opposite direction! Change!

Jesus said, "I do not bring peace of mind. I come not bringing peace but a sword." And with that sword, He would divide us from some things. He would cleave us from our possessions; He would cleave us from our comforts; He would cleave us from our shallow use of Christianity for our own selfish purposes. If we are ever to enter His kingdom, we must open ourselves to a larger knowledge of who we can become, and we must change. Change! Turn around! Repent!

Some people have the eternal struggle with calories or tobacco or alcohol. Those are nothing compared with total and radical spiritual change. We do not accomplish it by mouthing a bunch of words. We do it by opening ourselves to the power of God's Spirit, allowing God's Spirit to touch us and direct us and outfit us for this Kingdom we would find. We do it by deserting the inhibiting faith agendas and taking those deliberate steps which draw us into a larger spiritual process. We do it by saying in our heart of hearts, "Not my will but thine!"

Join me in completing this picture of who we are. An escaped prisoner has broken free and is running beside a stream, attempting to evade and outdistance his captors. He can hear the baying of the hounds far behind him. They are relentless. No matter how fast he runs or how far he gets, they are on his trail. They are trained to hunt him down, to follow the scent until they find him. His hope of escape is over-shadowed by his knowledge of how it will end. As long as he runs, they will pursue. It is only a matter of time.

Suddenly he stops! He listens to gauge the time and distance! Then he strikes out along the sandy bank, making visible and distinguishable tracks as he goes, careful to leave his imprint where it can be plainly seen. After losing most of his lead and wasting much of the precious-little time, he begins to make backward steps in his own tracks. Slowly and cautiously, he places one foot behind the other, bringing each down into a previous footprint. Back and back he goes, backward in the direction of the hounds. They are closer! He can hear the breaking of brush and the shouts of the handlers. He does not waver! Back he goes until he reaches the place where a low limb hangs above. In the din of voices and cries, just before they burst onto the scene, he leaps from the path and uses the limb to vault him far to the side and makes his escape.

We who are prisoners of this world must be no less wise. The hounds of the world are on our heels. They are relentless. No matter how far or how fast we run, no steps in any direction will free us from their pursuit. Our only hope of escape lies in the backward steps which seem so futile but which, in time, enable us to make the leap to real freedom. In that moment of abandonment, we engage God's moment, and we are not far from the Kingdom of God.

ALWAYS ON THE ROAD
Luke 9:1-6

And he called the twelve together and gave them power and authority over all demons and to cure diseases, and he sent them out to preach the kingdom of God and to heal. And he said to them, 'Take nothing for your journey, no staff, nor bag, nor bread, nor money; and do not have two tunics. And whatever house you enter, stay there, and from there depart. And wherever they do not receive you, when you leave that town shake off the dust from your feet as a testimony against them.' And they departed and went through the villages, preaching the gospel and healing everywhere. (Luke 9:1-6)

What is the Kingdom of God like? Is it like a cramped and narrow street down which only a select few will walk, or is it like a sprawling country estate with spacious grounds and adequate accommodations for all? Is it like a tunnel through which one must grope, seeking the light believed to be at the other end, or is it like the dazzling brightness of a celestial day? Who has not speculated about mansions in the skies or a shining city in the East and asked himself if this is not what the Kingdom of God must be like?

Of all that can be said about the Kingdom of God, perhaps the statements recorded in the gospels say it best. In Mark we read the words: "It is like a man going on a journey, when he leaves home and puts his servants in charge." *(13:34)*. In Matthew can be found the words, "For it will be as when a man going on a journey called his servants and entrusted to them his property ..." *(24:14)*. The same scriptures which urge us to seek, first of all, the Kingdom of God, describe it, not as a place but as a pilgrimage.

The Kingdom of God is like going on a journey. It is best characterized in all of the anticipation and the excitement and the preparation of a person about to take a trip.

Trips always have that lure and luster about them, whether they are for business or pleasure. There is with each of them the exhilaration of beginning something new and different, born from ancient and practiced enthusiasm. Every trip, however brief or incidental, places us upon the same high road of adventure, turning us from what is familiar and propelling us into the never-before-experienced circumstances for which we were created. Whether we go to Europe or to the grocery store, there is a little of the Gypsy in us all. We share in our hearts a fascination for trips. What would life be like without them?

Once when my kids were small, we planned a five hour trip with the three of them, and we decided to get underway before morning and spare ourselves some of the unnecessary conversation and the heat of the day. Placing them in the car in their pajamas, still sleeping, we were off without any commotion or conversation. And just as we left the city limits, moments from the time we pulled out of the driveway, one of them peeped over the seat with wide expectant eyes to ask that perennial question, "Are we there yet?" And then added, much to my surprise, "If we're not, would you like to hear a story?"

If you have ever looked forward to taking a trip, hear this story of what the Kingdom of God is like. It is all of the eagerness and suspense and desire that is associated with going on a journey, and it is ours for the taking. The mood of all who follow Christ is this same kind of excitement about the spiritual journey. Into all that is commonplace and familiar and dull in this existence, Jesus Christ presents an option which is bursting with promise and expectation, and which offers spiritual adventure beyond the home, beyond the sanctuary, beyond the selective relationships with family and friends.

When Jesus charged those first twelve with authority and power and sent them forth to heal and to preach the Kingdom of God, the conditions of their discipleship were incredible. "Take nothing with you," He told them. And so they went, without food or clothing, without money or weapons or belongings. They were instructed to receive hospitality where it was offered, making no preferences of their own, and to dismiss all negative encounters from their minds, lest they become discouraged and dissuaded from their mission.

We who read their story and are acquainted with their fellowship on the open road are sufficiently impressed by all that they did, yet never for a moment could we envision such a thing happening to us. Because it is unthinkable that we could dismiss from our lives our property, our business, our place in our families and our communities, the Kingdom of God is also unthinkable.

Christ does not require or command us to live a vagabond existence, we say. And He doesn't, in the body! But He does in the spirit! Only the person who is ready and willing to drop at a moment's notice all that he is doing in order to go somewhere spiritually will inherit the Kingdom of God. Only the church which is willing to be sent out into the world at the expense of its provincial mentality shall be counted worthy of the Kingdom of God. When the wind of the spirit blows, one is apt to bolt the doors and fasten the windows rather than permit its breeze to stir and move one in bold new directions.

What is meant by a faith that would take us places? What are its new directions? How do we define them? How will we know what they are? They will become apparent, not as we think and pray, but as we go and leave behind the bulk of everything we know. As we do, we shed the dead leaves of a cultural Christianity, and we notice these emerging buds: excellence without ego, serenity without separateness, friendship (to the point of a blending of souls) without fear.

The reason that many people and many churches are not going anywhere spiritually is that there is no assessment of where they are, no excitement and no adventure in their rigid and confining faith. It doesn't take them any of these places. The imagination is not captured, the pulse is not quickened, the heart is not stirred. There is no risk, no challenge, no horizon. It is religion tied with a string and labeled, "Fragile! Handle with Care!" But the label should read, "Urgent! Rush! Send at Once!"

The experience of surgery is perhaps the closest people come to the kind of excitement and abandon characteristic of the spiritual journey. The anticipation and dread of the unknown, the anxiety about the outcome, the fear of dying, the thrill of importance, the unbridled curiosity about what will happen —no rings, no jewelry, no glasses, no dentures —only the urgency of the trip defines the experience.

"Take nothing with you for your journey; no staff, nor bag, nor bread, nor money, nor clothes..." How tremendous it would be to stand as willing and as ready to obey the Lord as to obey the doctor or nurse. But most of us never follow Christ's directive. How tragic it is to deliberately miss the Kingdom of God. One can live right, pray a lot, sit in church, trust God, and miss it as completely as one would doing the opposite of all those things. It is the great journey of the Spirit for which one must be willing to forsake everything. It must have priority. It must be sought after, prayed for, lived for. When it is all these things, it moves us toward the presence of God.

The Kingdom of God is like going on a journey, leaving behind all that one has, but finding as one goes, every fulfillment that such a journey promises. One of them is **the freedom of the spirit**, freedom to be the person God wants us to be, freedom to do what God wants us to do. Such freedom is responsible to our spirits and not to our possessions.

If you could look out the porthole of a space capsule and view the earth, gleaming back at you like a cat's eye marble, what you left back there in your dresser drawer or in your suitcase would be infinitely less important than it is now. But looking a little closer at how we live, who mentally calculates the property boundaries or the home ownership of all that is seen in a blur as one travels the highways at lightning speed?

There is a tremendous freedom from concerns over terrestrial burdens when one embarks on the spiritual journey. It grows in direct proportion to the distance one places between himself and a stagnant and materialistic life. How refreshing to feel more responsibility for one's spirit than for one's possessions!

One of the provisions of the spiritual journey is the freedom of the spirit. Another is **the companionship of Christ.** The same Jesus who told his disciples to take nothing with them reminded them constantly that He would be with them wherever they were. His presence can be counted on in all of the ventures made in His name. It is as available today as it was when He accompanied His own disciples on the Emmaus Road.

Many who seek the Kingdom of God have to hang their heads in sorrow and turn away because they cannot abide the loneliness of the journey. The distance that it places between them and their friends and their neighbors is too great a price to pay. At the risk of deliberately missing the Kingdom, they will choose the world which urges them to call this journey off.

In one of his books, Louis L'Amour tells of a family arriving on the barren plains of the West to take up homesteading miles away from any neighbors. The husband, on a trip to a settlement, is killed. His wife toils away at her chores month after month, vainly awaiting his return. As she and her little children continue to scratch out a living there in the vast and empty land of the west, loneliness overwhelms her. It becomes so intense that on the long winter nights, when the wind is screaming outside the cabin, she writes brief notes and goes outside and attaches them to the rolling tumbleweeds, in vain hope that some wandering person will find them and read them. One of the messages went like this: "It is very cold, and I am often alone here. How I wish someone would come." *(L'Amour, p. 126).*

The spiritual journey gets lonely at times, and the temptation is never to take a step beyond one's social circle or become out of step with one's world. No one wants to pay the price of loneliness, a price that will come due the moment it is decided to walk a different road.

According to Einstein's Theory of Relativity, if you and I could leave this planet at a given speed and return a few days later, it would be a few years later by everybody else's clock. In fact, such a journey could easily place you in the same generation of your great grandchildren at the precise age you are now. If you can imagine how displaced you would be and how different you would feel about the world, you have some idea about the spiritual journey. It is characterized by this kind of loneliness.

Nothing on this journey is as exciting as who's along. You and I will never become lonely unless we forget the friend we have in Jesus. His companionship is promised, His fellowship is provided, His counsel is offered at every turn of the road and every dividing of the path. The farther we remove ourselves from the influences of the world, the greater His influence is in our lives. He travels this road, too, giving encouragement and support with each step.

The Kingdom of God is like a journey, and provision has been made for the vital things which are necessary and essential for its success. One is given freedom and companionship and is promised **a direction that leads to God.** So many choices are before us every day we live. So many directions create their perpetual options in your life and mine. But the direction is clear from the beginning: "Seek ye first the Kingdom of God, and all of these things will be added unto you."

Nothing turned Christendom upside down as much as the quest for the Holy Grail. Knights in every realm galloped in all directions, pursuing whatever logical courses they felt would lead them to the desired object. Each knight dreamed of finding the cup which had touched the Master's lips that night of the Last Supper. Codes of honor and chivalry were once again established and upheld; purity and nobility became the virtues of every knight; humility and integrity existed beneath every piece of armor. It was believed that none but the pure in heart would ever find the Grail.

So far as anyone knows, the Grail was never found, but the generation of wandering knights errant it created amazed, defied, and changed the world. The object of the Quest wasn't that essential. It was the quest itself which was of consequence.

The direction that leads to God isn't to be taken for a crown or a halo or any other object. It is to be taken for the journey itself. The values of it will emerge in the process, values which will awe and defy and change our world and make us fit for the Kingdom we would find.

Seeking the Kingdom of God is like going on a journey, leaving behind all that one has, but finding as one goes, the freedom of the spirit, the companionship of Christ, and the direction which leads to God. Do not make the mistake of settling for less and deliberately missing it. There is much which is important and worthwhile, but the journey is everything.

Sources:

Louis L'Amour. Conagher. Bantam Books. New York, NY. 1982. p. 126.

TRAVELING LIGHT
Luke 9:57-58

As they were going along the road, a man said to him, "I will follow you wherever you go." And Jesus said to him, "Foxes have holes, and birds of the air have nests; but the Son of man has no place to lay his head."
(Luke 9:57-58)

Howard and Harriet Sizemore weren't the typical sweepstakes winners. Howard never paid attention to the attractive junk mail or gave much credence to the philosophy that one could get something for nothing. He had even grumbled the day Harriet sent back the return letter, complaining that it was a waste of postage. Harriet wasn't a great believer, herself, but, for once, she felt that the price of a stamp was worth a shot at all that money. After all, they might get lucky.

The Sizemores did get lucky; incredibly lucky. They became first place winners in that very sweepstakes and were given their choice of receiving all of the money at one time or so much a month for the rest of their lives. Both admitted that they never dreamed they would actually win, and that they had not decided what to do about the money. "It really is a problem," Howard said. "You think that when something like this happens, your worries are over and you're fixed for life, but it is more complicated than that."

Most of us do not have to win a sweepstakes to realize how mythological it is to be "fixed for life." If money is the magic solution many believe it to be, none of us should have any problems. We've got more of it than we have ever had in our lives, and we can turn the clock back just a few years and remember when we had nowhere near as much. Affluence has come so rapidly that people who were as poor as dirt have gone out and bought themselves "pieces of the rock." Practically all of us have come into a windfall, yet our worries are not over; our lives are not any less complicated; we don't breathe or sleep easier. We've bought the myth, and some of us are still looking to receive, any day, that letter which announces us as winners.

Many people really believe that money is the answer to their problems. They don't profess that in their conversations, but they demonstrate it with their lives, and they are counting on it so heavily that they refuse to believe anyone could convince them otherwise. Yet there is One who can. Before you buy anything else, before you open a new account, you need to realize that, long ago, a man named Jesus shattered the myth.

Into a world where it was business as usual, Jesus came, offering the adventure of a lifetime. He had no money, no reputation, no backing, but He fascinated others in a way which compelled them to follow Him. He promised neither possessions nor positions nor privileges, but to every person He encountered, He gave willingly of himself. His was a strange imprudent notion — spend, scatter, give away! Some paid no heed, but some left everything to follow Him.

Picture them going with Him through a grainfield, plucking at random from the heads of grain and eating as they went, completely mobile and attached to nothing but the irresistible urge to participate in His life and His ministry. Breaking out of their oppressive structures, leaving behind their sedentary lifestyles, they went out into the world and shared with everyone they met this new life which they found in Him.

This same Jesus bids you and me follow! Do we dare change from our static postures? Do we dare abandon our entrenched position? A place with Christ requires that we be ready and willing to move from where we are to follow where He leads. We cannot go anywhere "holed up" in a fortress faith.

Many churches are sitting in their places, wondering what is going to happen when they should be going places making things happen. Why are they content to remain where they are? The answer is easy. They are simply magnifying the minds and hearts of multitudes who will not leave everything and follow! Our churches are in danger of becoming anachronistic outposts which are no longer nomadic with their witness.

One of the toys my children got for Christmas when they were little was called a "Sit n Spin." To operate it, one of them had to sit on a large disk and turn a smaller disk by hand. This turning rotated the large disk and spun the child around until he grew dizzy or got tired of turning the small disk. The"Sit n Spin" did precisely what the name said. One sat, one spun, yet the toy never moved from its fixed position. The "Sit n Spin" is characteristic of the entrenched faith. It is capable of movement, it gives the sensation of going somewhere, yet it only takes its occupants in circles, not directions.

For our faith to take us places, it must find a place with Christ. A place with Christ is not a fixed position. It is by His side as He goes. Christ urges us to drop whatever it is we are doing and go with Him. We cannot take along the old mentality. There is no room for our cumbersome structures and our materialistic values. Christ cautions all who would follow Him to travel light, leaving behind every vestige of their religious decadence. Christ would have us cast aside our compromised theology and take His gospel and run with it.

If you have bought the myth of affluence and have been disillusioned by its extravagant promises; if you have reached the point where you have begun to doubt the "quick fix" solutions assured by money in all of its attractive and acceptable applications, allow me to acquaint you with a once in a lifetime opportunity. You could be a winner in the most important sweepstakes that will ever be held in your lifetime, but the prize is not money. The prize is a trip to anywhere you want to go, but listen to the conditions: You furnish your own transportation. You pay your own expenses. You take your own chances. The rest has been arranged. You can stay as long as you like. You don't ever have to come back. Don't miss this exciting offer. Commit your life to Jesus Christ and go right now!

Jesus Christ is your host on the spiritual journey, and as your host, He has worked out the agenda of it for you, along with a list of reminders so that you will not forget the numerous details involved. Listen to the most important one: "Foxes have holes, and birds of the air have nests; but the Son of Man has nowhere to lay His head." That is the most important because, after it registers its impact in the average mind and heart, many who have signed up will not want to go.

We like to think that no one but a fool would ever refuse a personal invitation from Christ to go out into the world with Him, but there were many who, for various reasons, would not accompany Him. These same reasons prevail today in the decision to remain behind. Consider them as we discuss three aspects of the trip which greatly limit its appeal and its popularity.

The Spiritual Journey will not wait. Time does not permit its postponement. The clock is running. There will never be a more convenient to take it than right now. It is a trip which cannot be rescheduled whatever the reason. If we go, we must go now.

George Washington was a stickler for punctuality. If any invited guests straggled in late, Washington was likely to tell them, "Gentlemen, I have a cook who never asks whether the company has come but whether the hour has come." *(RD, 1963, p. 182).*

The hour came for one young man who wanted to go with Jesus, but he wanted to delay it until a later time. "Lord, let me first go and bury my father." His logic was reasonable! His excuse was perfect, but the journey would not wait for him, and it will not wait for us.

I watched my younger son on the basketball court. His team was behind by eight points. It was frustrating for him and his teammates to stand poised and ready while the other team dribbled and passed, dribbled and passed. They were running down the clock. Any desperate attempt to break that monotony would result in a foul and a likely free throw for the opposing team. What fueled the desperation was not just being behind in the score. The larger part of the frustration was having to play a team that considered "waiting it out" as a strategy for winning.

The world is poised and ready! What about the Church? If it is to live and move in the name of Christ as the physical empowerment of His spiritual presence, it cannot do so by running down the clock. For the Church to rescue the world from the host of competing alternatives which would further entrap it and corrupt it and defile it, it must act now! There may be excellent reasons for delay, but this is an opportunity that will not wait.

An opportunity is before you to respond to the personal invitation of Jesus Christ and go with Him, but only when you resolve to go unencumbered from all that would hold you back can you keep pace with Him. You don't have forever to make up your mind. The spiritual journey will not wait; and, secondly, **it does not vary.**

Life is a smorgasbord existence. It is difficult to decide what is the most important and what must have priority. The committed Christian does not have the luxury of debate. The journey Christ would have us take with Him must be first and foremost. It cannot be rerouted to accommodate lesser aims. Another young man who wanted to go with Jesus would have been instantly included, but another commitment took precedence. "Let me first say farewell to those at my home," he said. His willingness to accompany Christ was secondary to other interests, but the journey did not vary for him, and it does not vary for us.

James C. Dobson's celebrated film series, "Focus on the Family," has been acclaimed by many church groups as one of the best things done to bolster Christian family life. He relates in one of the films how he repeatedly told parents to spend more time with their kids. Lecturing on this topic and writing numerous books which encourage this special personal interaction, he realized at one point that he wasn't spending enough time with his kids. He was so busy telling others what they should do that his own message could not get through to him.

Isn't that the character of most religious activity? The great merits of the faith have been subordinated to chatter and verbiage until only the information about them is experienced and not the merits themselves. Christ would have his people move from the platitudes to the activity by inviting them to go with Him. It is a lot easier to talk about it, but regardless of how one tries to reduce the journey to the armchair, it does not vary.

A place with Christ is not a fixed position. It is by His side as He goes, completely mobile and attached to nothing but the irresistible urge to participate in His life and His love. You can deliberate forever about your ability to do that, but the journey will not wait; it does not vary; and, finally, **it allows no extras.** There is no room for excess baggage of any kind, especially that having to do with old attitudes and old behaviors. If one goes, he must travel light, taking nothing that adds extra weight

Out of the corner of my eye while huffing around a walking track at 5:00 a.m., I noticed something sprinkled on the gravel. On the next lap, I paused and stooped down to see what it was. There were the remnants of a bag of french fries. Someone had obviously eaten them while moving at a good clip, for a piece or two gleamed out of the dark for the next twenty or thirty yards. Imagine someone dedicated enough to burn the calories and the fat and, at the same time, wolfing down one of the very things motivating the exercise. What a marvelous insight into the great American passion for having it both ways.

A third young man who wished to accompany Jesus shared that same passion and had to remain behind. He was burdened down with possessions. Jesus said to him, "Sell what you have and give it to the poor; and come, and follow me." But the young man could not do it. Though his life was commendable in every other respect, the journey allowed no extras for him, and it allows none for us.

Only when one goes through the world unencumbered and unburdened by pre-conceived attitudes can he go with the Christ who beckons him to follow. "Foxes have holes, birds of the air have nests, but the Son of man has nowhere to lay his head." Knowing that, will you go with Him or will you decide to remain behind?

One of the best images of our tradition is that of the circuit rider traveling on horseback with no possessions other than those in his saddlebags. It is a comforting image of a dedicated veteran with a portable means to convey a timeless message. Behind the image, however, are startling and exhilirating contradictions which rescue it from its assigned spiritual complacency.

A young man would be touched at a meeting, his society would recommend him, and he would be off, sometimes immediately, to follow the circuit rider and assume the status of a junior preacher. At the conference, he would be appointed to some distant field and strike out for it the day the conference concluded. No home to live in, no worldly goods, no training beyond the burning zeal to go and preach the gospel. Nowhere in the great passion of that decision was there a thought of giving up or going back. All of life was predicated on a moment in a meeting when heart and mind and soul and strength were galvanized and forever changed.

In a moment, you and I come to that decision in our lives when we must ratify our total religious experience and go with the Christ who bids us follow or else remain behind. The moment comes so quickly, and you recognize it the instant it arrives. In that moment, it is easier to go than it is to apologize profusely once the moment passes.

Sources:

Reader's Digest. Reader's Digest Assoc. Inc. Pleasantville, NY. March, 1963, p. 182.

LOST IN PASSING
Luke 10:30-32

"A man was going down from Jerusalem to Jericho, and he fell among robbers, who stripped him and beat him, and departed, leaving him half dead. Now by chance, a priest was going down that road; and when he saw him he passed by on the other side. So likewise a Levite, when he came to the place and saw him, passed by on the other side. (Luke 10:30-32)

The time is 1873. The place is London. A man named Phileas Fogg has just accepted a wager to journey around the world in slightly less than three months, an almost impossible feat, and report back by the deadline or else forfeit the wager. Taking with him his French valet and a detective assigned by his opponents to check up on his movements, Fogg, the typical methodical Englishman, starts out on his impossible trip.

Adventure is piled on adventure, but the intrepid Englishman overcomes every obstacle to his journey with endless resourcefulness. Fighting mobs in one place, rescuing a beautiful woman from death in another, Fogg maintains his timetable despite incredible odds. At the end of the journey, he walks into the room where the wager had been made ten minutes ahead of schedule, as the waiting group looks at their watches. Thus ends the famous novel by Jules Verne called, *Around the World in Eighty Days*. (f. *Dictionary of Great Book Digests,* p. 1609).

Jules Verne was one of the great companions of my childhood. His books, though a century old, were packed with excitement and adventure which had entertained more than one generation of young readers. Stories like *20,000 Leagues Under the*

Sea, From the Earth to the Moon, A Journey to the Center of the Earth, were but a few of his thrilling tales. Practically every story described a breath-taking trip of such importance that characters and plots were secondary in comparison. The journeys were all-consuming, dwarfing all of the circumstances around them. They were often taken and continued at the risk and even at the expense of the people involved.

If that sounds like a lot of early science-fiction to you, brace yourself. Countless Christian people have this same all-consuming passion about the spiritual journey they are taking. It means more to them than anything else. Such is their commitment to it that nothing must interfere or disrupt their schedule. No one must stand in the way! There is no time to waste on anyone or anything, so urgent is the necessity to be on one's way.

The journey to the presence of God is important, more important than any other journey we will take. It must have priority. It must captivate us to the extent that we will allow nothing to prevent our going, but therein lies the danger. When our preoccupation with the journey becomes so total that we deny room in our lives for the people who insist that we stop and help them; that we stop and listen to them; that we stop and encounter and encourage and embrace them, we, who are in such a haste to go on to perfection, become lost in passing.

Compassion for people is an essential attribute for those who seek the Kingdom of God. It's great to deny oneself, to perfect oneself, to project one's self, but the real progress made on the spiritual journey depends upon the exchanges which take place with the people one meets and passes along the way. Whatever our urgency, we should find time for people and not rush past them or over them to make it farther and faster ourselves.

Downtown congregations are always in danger of the"wrong persons" wandering in: the drunk who finds his way to the line of the family night dinner, the panhandler who waits outside to hit on the Sunday crowd, the homeless woman who slips into an eleven o'clock service and causes ripples in the pew.

The Levite in us all would have us target and expel these and others in order to feel comfortable or validated or distinguished in our Christianity. How terribly absurd!

A church I have served is in a community historically known for its mental institution. For some years now, many who have been treated there have become part of the community. Some make a better go of it than others. One young man with quite volatile behavior found a home with us each Sunday morning for a number of months. Members introducing themselves to him would be met with a response like, "I'm very glad to meet you! My name is Jesus Christ!" At times, he could create a disturbance by sitting with the acolytes at the very front and mimicking my movements in the pulpit for all to see. Though it drove some of the ushers right up the wall, how refreshing it was to have someone illustrate to us the fun God must have with our piety and our decorum through the medium of a "wrong person" or a fleeting onetime relationship.

If anybody knew about the stigma of "wrong persons" and the value of a onetime relationship, it was Jesus Christ. He associated with so-called "wrong persons". He changed the world, but He did it one person at a time. A lot of preachers would like to change the world, and some of them think they can do it from large pulpits and civic auditoriums and television. Not one of them thinks he can do it one person at a time! Jesus Christ changed the world because He respected every person, and He knew the value of a one-to-one relationship. Always conscious of the journey He was making, He always found time for people, and the journey was enhanced because of it.

With all the other insights you and I have into His story about the Good Samaritan, we must consider it in light of the premium he placed on the one-to-one relationship. The story concerns a man in trouble and two obvious choices for helping him: the Priest and the Levite, orthodox Jews compelled by their teachings to love their neighbor. But in the end, it is the less obvious choice, the Samaritan, who actually stops and helps.

Without taking anything away from the Samaritan who helped, what was the problem with the obvious choices? Religious men, committed men, seeking, no doubt, that city without foundations, willing to do all that was required to inherit eternal life, but insensitive and without compassion for one lying helpless by the side of the road. The poignant thing about their problem is that they are so typical of the obvious choices today.

Travel in this country is so fast-paced that we can go from one end to the other without seeing very much. We can put hundreds of miles behind us and be oblivious to the surroundings. The concentration on the dull gray strip with the white line broken by the anonymity of countless vehicles promises us a monotonous and impersonal trip to wherever it is we are going. Spiritual travel can be like that! We can be in the driver's seat in our complacent little lives, obeying all the rules, moving right along in the passing lane, putting the years behind us as we become more conscientious about righteousness and our relation to it — and miss the whole point of the trip.

Christian people are the obvious choices in a world littered from one end to the other with casualties of every type. Even within our own communities, where the casualties have names and faces familiar to us, the insensitivity is appalling. Check the track record of any church in relation to the crises in its own backyard, and the apathy you encounter will stun you. We're leaving a lot of people by the side of the road, and we are the obvious choice.

The Priest and the Levite have become the prototypes for the modern pilgrimage of faith. Their semiconscious witness is characteristic of the witness of so many Christian people whose patent concerns for the world and those in it fail to provide any real assistance. Their virtuous hesitation to intercede in the human situation is mirrored in today's successful Christian life.

Nothing causes God more embarrassment than one of His religious elites grinning down from a spiritual plateau upon the struggling and sinful lower forms, proud of himself for having transcended their level and for having arrived at such a lofty vantage point. The euphoria can hardly be contained as he thinks in his heart, "I've made it, and look at them! I have surpassed them all!" and, turning his back upon the wretched state of affairs beneath him, he continues his climb.

The well-worn phrase of T.S. Eliot's is a sufficient commentary on anyone's journey.

> The last temptation is the greatest treason
> To do the right thing for the wrong reason.

Unworthy ambitions prevent us from being a help along the way, and there are three of them which are likely to be encountered on the spiritual journey, ranging in intensity from subtle to glaring. They are pride, indifference and deceit, but rarely are they recognized as such. So that they might be more easily identified as the results of unworthy ambitions, more sympathetic categories are needed. They are presented to you almost apologetically, in hopes that they do not apply, but with the sobering knowledge that they probably do. Going the full extent to spare as much pain as possible, let us label the first category, **the wrong way to do right.**

Those who attempt to follow the commandments of God are doing the right thing. In the accomplishment of it, however, there is the temptation to save oneself and to feel no responsibility for anyone else's salvation. A premium is placed on personal progress, and the journey is accelerated to the point that it is exclusively and uniquely one's own. Everybody else is expendable.

Picture the priest, probably on his way to some ecclesiastic duty, spying the victim by the road but deciding to avoid him. A priest had to keep himself pure. Contact with a corpse or with a person about to become one would defile him for seven days. He could not afford to waste seven precious days decontaminating. His priestly duties came first! He went his way, wrongly doing the right thing.

It was in a surburb of Atlanta near one of the interstate exits during Holy Week. Invited by a church in the area, a young minister was on his way from across town to deliver a short sermon during a mid-week luncheon. An automobile accident which had just occurred threatened to block his path and make him late. He felt fear in the pit of the stomach, not for the victims of the accident but for the fact that he might be delayed. Against his better judgment and without a thought as to who might be hurt in either vehicle in front of him, he swerved out to get around the accident scene before the road became blocked off. As he did, he almost clipped an injured child who was emerging from one of the wrecked cars. A policeman arriving on the scene immediately pulled him over and placed him in the back seat of his cruiser. Needless to say, he missed his speaking engagement, but imagine his explanation to the officer as to why he exercised such reckless disregard. "I had a sermon to deliver, and these people were in my way . . ."

It is the unworthy ambitions which complicate the journey and pose problems. They cannot be completely avoided, but they can be effectively resisted if we will find the time for the people we discover along the way. Having identified one result of unworthy ambition as the wrong way to do right, let us label a second category, **the safe way to be good.**

The Levite walking on the road was a good man. He was of the priestly family by that name, a family much admired for its concern with spiritual matters. The concern did not extend to the victim lying by the side of the road because it was too risky to become involved with such people. One could get in over his head by not knowing with whom he was actually dealing. Better safe than sorry. He went his way, in his selective goodness, confident that he had decided wisely in the matter.

The address of a new family who had visited with the church was near the location of a lake quite a distance from town. My Administrative Board chairman for that year lived in the same vicinity and offered to ride with me and guide me to their house for a visit. It was during the Christmas season. Darkness came early. It was good to have him along since that particular area was unfamiliar to me at night.

As we topped the last rise getting to this remote destination, the black sky was aglow with reflections. Pulling up to the driveway, what greeted us was a double-wide mobile home with

Christmas lights strung over every possible square inch of it. The yard was fairly littered with beer cans and beer bottles, and loud music and argumentative voices were coming from the open front door. I recognized the tune as "Blue Christmas," sung by Elvis. This scene was about 180 degrees from what either of us expected. As someone from the inside walked to the door, I told my companion that I would only be a minute and asked him to step out with me to greet this family. He shook his head in the negative and said he would wait for me. I asked him a second and third time to join me just to extend a cordial hand of welcome. Still, he refused. Finally, I asked, "What's the problem?" And he said, "I don't have enough money for the jukebox!" And he remained in the car during that brief visit.

The Levite in us wants to be good, but the line is drawn at the limit of personal safety. The creed is well-worn and tiresome. "Better safe than sorry!" Yet genuine goodness is courageous and engaging. It does not take shelter; it takes charge. It recognizes the worth of every person, and it always extends the helping hand. Those possessing such goodness have never met a "wrong person".

On the spiritual journey, it is the consequences of unworthy ambitions which prevent us from being a help along the way. Because of them, little or no provision is made for people, and there is the danger of becoming lost in passing. We've discussed the wrong way to do right; the safe way to be good; let us label the third category: **the small way to stand out.**

The Priest and the Levite were the obvious choices, but the victim by the road revealed the truth about them. His situation required a response in character with the life-style they professed, but these two righteous persons not only passed him by but did it from the other side of the road.

There is a sign in a Kentucky cabinet shop which reads, "Genuine antiques made here." That advertisement is similar to the standards carried by many pretenders to the throne of grace who pilfer the witness of the Christian community, displacing much that is authentic and valuable in its profession of faith.

Once when my wife was hospitalized, she was fortunate to have the prayers and support of numerous visitors. One of these was a minister who stopped by and met her for the first time. Around his neck was a huge metal cross which, because of its size, was an almost impractical burden; nevertheless, it soundly identified its wearer who bore it piously. Before leaving the room, he offered to have a prayer, and as he leaned over her bedside, the pendulum motion of that imposing cross was such that it struck full force against my wife's head.

The journey should never become so obsessive that it is undertaken at the risk and even at the expense of people. Compassion for people, time for them, concern with their struggles is central to this search for the Kingdom of God. To stay on track, one must refrain from totally preoccupying oneself with what lies ahead and forever scan the side of the road for those who have stumbled and fallen by the way.

Sources:

William Barclay. Daily Study Bible. The Westminster Press. Philadelphia. 1956. Luke, pp. 141-142.
Richard Bielski. (owner of) Dictionary of Great Book Digests. p. 1609.
T.S. Eliot. The Complete Poems & Plays. Harcourt. Brace & Co, New York. 1952. p. 196.

MADE FOR MORE
John 14:12-14

"Truly, truly, I say to you, he who believes in me will also do the works that I do; and greater works than these will he do, because I go to the Father. Whatever you ask in my name, I will do it, that the Father may be glorified in the Son; if you ask anything in my name, I will do it." (John 14: 12-14)

One of the most famous and successful of medieval European travelers was Marco Polo. This young Venetian left Italy with his father and two uncles and journeyed to the Far East. For three and a half years they travelled across Asia and came at length to the court of Kublai Khan. For seventeen additional years, Marco Polo experienced the wonders of this strange and exotic land. He was a man in middle age when he returned to Italy, brimming with stories of the Orient. He told of stones that would burn, powder that would explode, customs and clothing so foreign to the European taste that they were thought to be preposterous. Marco Polo, because of his adventures, had made hundreds of exciting discoveries the average listener found hard to believe. In fact, nobody really believed him until centuries later when his discoveries were confirmed by other travelers.

Can you imagine the sadness and the frustration that come in trying to convince someone else that there is more to life than the life he knows, that there is more to the world than her familiar corner of it, that there are beyond one's comprehension greater things to comprehend, only to have someone say, "I don't believe you"? If you can imagine it, then you know some of the frustration that documents the spiritual journey. The insights and discoveries which are gained on the way to the presence of God are so out of context with most of what is routinely experienced that they cannot be effectively communicated. Even in those rare instances when communication takes place, those who listen find it hard to believe.

The skeptics of today are of a different sort. The great difficulty faced in presenting a sufficient and convincing witness to the world is that an amazing number of "closet" non-believers are the churched. Bogged down in spiritless complacency, thoroughly convinced that faith is simply a process of adaptation, many Christian congregations have never scratched the surface of their possibilities. There is more to be discovered than has been surmised and settled for, but who would believe it? There is greater involvement awaiting the faithful outside the sanctuary, but who remains convinced? Our churches continue to cherish their traditions and their sterile community-related roles, but the question is, "Are they Christ-effective?"

The spirit of Christ is adventurous in nature, liberating in intention, exploratory by definition. To be in Christ is to be compelled to go where His spirit takes us. Christ needs no more unimaginative participants with folded hands in well-worn pews. He needs modern day Marco Polos who will dare to step beyond the present translations of their faith and bring back fresh bold interpretations, and who will make countless repeated attempts to convert the world to what they are. To be Christ-effective, one must be willing to discover and endorse the possibilities beyond the boundaries of the customary witness in Jesus' name and for His sake.

Years ago, when I was a member of a church staff, one of my duties was to give tours through the building to any group who happened to visit us. Since the building was somewhat of an architectural novelty, people came through its doors simply to look at its design or at its beautiful stained-glass windows. On one occasion, I was leading a group of young school children through, showing them the Bride's Room and the Robing Room and various classrooms. We entered a landing with a circular staircase that spiraled to an old sacristy, which at the time was empty. It was a particularly dark area of the building. One little child at the front of the line looked up at me with wide eyes and asked, "Is this where they keep the bodies?"

You and I have been duped into believing that we can build churches and sit in them; pay preachers and listen to them; be regular and attentive and generous with our money and equate that to mean that we are somehow about the gospel of Christ when, in reality, we are quite dead. If the spirit of Christ is in our churches, nothing about us or our buildings suggests a funeral atmosphere. There will be no restrictive perimeters sheltering soft music and do-nothing faith.

Christian congregations in America are idling with the motor running, and the only thing noticeable about them is an audible hum! It takes the spirit of the Master to give life and breath and vitality to every Christian enterprise. Without that spirit, the faith becomes a monotony of Sunday morning reruns and daily vignettes to be played back when the occasion suits. But with that spirit, it becomes an action-packed involvement which demands everything one has to give. With that spirit, people and churches move from who is willing to who will.

If you are one of the people who has never dared anything beyond prayer and public worship, let me be among the first to inform you that you were made for more. There is a journey awaiting you the moment you resolve to go that is unlike any you have ever taken before. It is a spiritual trek into life's unexplored territories for the purpose of gathering and bringing back all the information available —a reconnaissance mission, if you will! Bear in mind that prior to departure there is no training process, no waiting period, and no special skills required. The only qualification necessary is that one must be Christ-effective.

It was to Christ-effective young men that Jesus gave the promise of His spirit —willing men, who in His absence were resolved to carry out the assignments they had been given. It did not matter that they had never been where they were going, that they had never done what they were undertaking. They were convinced that this was the great purpose for which they were created, and they went, giving no thought to the magnitude of their own limitations. "Believe in me, and you will do the works that I do," He had told them. "And greater works than these will you do."

The Christ-effective life does not allow itself to become defeated by its own limitations. It does not limit itself to its religious experience or to its church affiliation. It is willing to explore. It is not confined to a home turf or a particular community. It will visit beyond the boundaries. It may find itself in some incredible places, but it is willing and resolved to go, flinging reservation to the wind, because it knows it was made for more.

In order to do the great works they were made for, Christian people are going to have to face some realities and admit that their outreach is ingrown. When churches feel more emotion for families in their cemetery than for those down the road in a trailer park, when they fellowship within a rock's throw of residents whose presence they have never acknowledged and whose homes they have never visited, it is time to rethink some strategies.

One can accomplish great things for Christ only when there is a willingness to **reach more in His name.** So many people within easy reach of Christian churches all over America are not being reached. Local churches everywhere are dying on the vine, not because people are unavailable to them, but because they are unavailable to people. If present limitations are to be overcome, Christ-effective people must resolve to reach more in His name.

In his book, *A Walk Across America,* Peter Jenkins describes the four month difficulty he had getting his body in shape for such a trip. "On July 5th," he said, "something happened that almost made me quit. It was over 90 degrees...Halfway up the mountain, I felt I was going to melt. Still, I forced myself to keep going ... Behind me I heard a light tapping on the pavement. It sounded as smooth and rhythmic as a thoroughbred trotting across the back stretch in a harness race. With a whoosh, a flash of bright-colored track shoes and long legs passed me as easy as a Mercedes passing a hay wagon...Seeing that effortless man flow by me made me want to quit right there."

Rather than undergo the rigors necessary to tone up and strengthen their witness so that it might move across this continent, many of the faithful have given up and called it quits. They are not reaching people because they have not conditioned themselves to go very far. They have not felt the compulsion to go where the journey takes them, and, clutching desperately to their little pieces of geography, they opt to be caretakers rather than trailblazers.

The spirit of the Master is central to the theme of any venture one accepts on His behalf. It provides the incentive needed to clear every hurdle in the path and the resilience to supersede all limitations, but it must be matched by a willingness to respond to its activity.

Great things for Christ are accomplished only when there is a willingness to reach more in His name, and having reached out, to **touch more in His love.** With their commercial jingle, "Reach out and touch someone," the telephone system has pinpointed a basic need that the Christian community should have identified and met long ago. People are lonely. They yearn for communication, for company, for comfort. Who is better equipped to touch them than Christ-effective people resolved to touch them in His love?

When Lewis and Clark scouted this country west of the Mississippi, they discovered that in many places they were the only Europeans the Indians had ever seen. The Indians took an instant liking to this small group because they were as mannerly, kind, and generous as any guests they had ever entertained. Willingly sharing food, medicine and modest gifts, Lewis and Clark, as representatives of their government, maintained good relations with the Indians while on their three year reconnoitering expedition and returned without the loss of a single life or the first incident of hostility.

All adventures come with the fright of not knowing what will happen or exactly who is out there or how they will react, but never to go is to scorn the possibilities within oneself for the achievement of great things. Jesus Christ will always call His people to do great things. His spirit will enable them to accomplish every task and overcome every limitation. Given that assurance, who can help but go? Who would dare remain behind? Against the drought of religious mediocrity, it is the challenges which supply the nectar all would drink, and the challenges facing the believers of Christ today are to reach more in His name, to touch more in His love, and to **heal more in His power.**

To be in Christ is to be ready, not only to do and to dare, but to instigate His healing in shattered and confused personalities, in battered families and broken homes, in the multitude of helpless and hopeless situations. To be in Christ is to possess His power within and His compassion without. The world doesn't need any more referral agencies. There is enough token concern already. What the world needs is for the members of the Christian community to recognize the power at their disposal and assume the stewardship of souls.

Well into the twentieth century people travelled long distances seeking mineral springs. The water from these springs was thought to have great medicinal value, and many regulars could attest to the benefits of daily consumption. Mineral springs can still be found throughout the country where their water is still available, but few people frequent them or use their refreshment. Historical markers identify them simply as antiquated sources of hope for a vanishing clientele.

Only Christ-effective people can dispel this same grim notion about the Church as they express their willingness to accomplish great things. "Believe in me," Jesus said, "and you will do the works that I do. And greater works than these will you do."

George Sheehan's book, *Running and Being,* describes a runner finding his or her second wind after reaching the point of exhaustion, when it looks and feels as if he or she can't go one foot more. In his description of this remarkable feature of our own physiology, Sheehan tells how a runner reaches that last long hill, rubbery-legged, and miraculously, begins to draw upon reserves of strength he hardly knew he possessed, and then says, "I know I am made for more!" *(Angell, p. 54).*

How tremendous it is to know that each person has the opportunity to do great things for Jesus Christ and to be an adventurer beyond the boundaries that are presently defined. Go, then! Resolve to go! Do not think about the difficulties! Go, even if you have to go alone. Give everything to it that you have, and there will be much to speak of when you return.

Sources:

James Angell. Adult Leader. Cokesbury. Nashville, TN. Mar-April-May, 1981, p. 54.
Peter Jenkins. A Walk Across America. Fawcett Book Group. New York, NY. p. 27.

THE LONGEST MILE
Matthew 5:41

"If any one forces you to go one mile, go with him two miles." (Matthew 5:41)

Every couple of years, Jerry gets a new pair of shoes, and it is always somewhat of a private emotional hassle for him to break them in. Jerry is a jogger, and he is educated when it comes to proper foot-gear. He knows that inferior running shoes will not only wreck his feet but damage his joints. He ran for years in poorly designed shoes, but now he wears only those which are of top quality and which are specially designed for the pounding that he gives them. The problem is that Jerry always hates to part with his old shoes when they become worn-down at the heels and the time has come for new ones.

It is almost a silly thing, but Jerry feels like he is ditching old friends when he has to change shoes. They are so comfortable, so perfect in their fit, molded after a year or two to his own gait and body pressure. It is a shame to toss them for a new pair. Each time he laces up a strange and alien pair, the difference is noticeable and sometimes a little awkward. There is always the subtle pang of wanting the old ones back, but Jerry has gone through the exchange ritual enough times to know that he can't run forever in worn-out shoes.

There are people just like Jerry who are on the spiritual journey. They have to make the inner and sometimes trivial decisions all the time which keep them fit for the road. Some of the things they think about and deliberate about are so slight, yet when overall performance is considered, they are part of the process which determines how everything eventually shakes out. It is amazing what minutiae go on in their heads which ultimately have a profound effect on the mileage they get out of the road. No one thing is too slight or too unimportant to be disregarded. That is just the way this particular journey works.

It is interesting that Jesus seemed unconcerned with such particulars when He made his pronouncement about going the extra mile as one of the ways to follow Him into the presence of God. This notion of the extra mile has become a popular phrase in churches who ask people to do a little more with their time or their giving or their attentiveness to certain concerns. It is a metaphor that has been domesticated to the point of being a harmless little homily, but it needs to be reconsidered by those who would dismiss it as one of life's many details. Being asked to go a mile in the days of Jesus was not the request of a lonely person or a petition made by a stranger unfamiliar with directions. It was generally the command of a soldier given at random to any person he selected to help him.

All Jews were under conscription in their relationship to the Romans who occupied their country. They could be pressed into service at any time and forced to carry messages or burdens for a distance by anyone who represented the Roman government. Being asked to go a mile was not a request but an order. One can see how the directive to go an extra mile would have startled the average listener standing there taking in Jesus's Sermon on the Mount.

Such a resolution to go two miles with someone forcing you to go one did not seem to have all the ingredients of a good idea. There was no way to feel good about the good one was doing. There was only outrage at being forced to comply against one's will, humiliation from having to demonstrate instant obedience, hatred for the verbal and physical abuse inflicted by discourteous and contemptible oppressors. It is in this hostile atmosphere and attitude that Jesus initiated a willingness not only to go the distance, but to go it twice over.

On the spiritual journey, every step is not voluntary. Those who follow Christ are sometimes asked to go part of the way in strange and different shoes. One cannot always follow and do as one pleases. The journey to the presence of God cannot be completed unless some conscription is imposed. There are no taskmasters on the spiritual journey pressing us into service. Conscription, when it is decreed, is something one imposes on oneself.

Plodding on, under duress by one's own hand, is the mark of true discipleship. If there is not within the Christian this capacity to force himself forward, Christ will only be followed so far. How one handles difficulties always determines the distance one will go. The degree of commitment required of oneself is the measure by which one advances or falls back, and if it is less than total, the journey is in doubt. On the spiritual journey the longest mile is the first mile, and **the conscription is self-imposed.**

Some of the visitation that pastors do would qualify as self-imposed conscription. Take the newcomer visitation when it quickly becomes apparent that those who signed the register and were open to a visit have only a utilitarian interest. The visit consists of a check-list of what is there for their children at church and what isn't. No response to the pastor's statements about ministry and service opportunities. No desire to learn more about the church. Just going down the aisle of a church like one would cruise the aisles of a department store. "Attention, church shoppers!"

On one such visit to a young man who had attended church that morning, I was invited into his apartment with a brisk wave of a hand and asked to take a seat. Before I could get a word out, he asked, "Do you have a singles program in your church?" I said, "Well, no, but we have a Sunday School class that . . ." He interrupted, "Do you have any group that meets in the evening where a single man might meet single women?" I said, "Well, no, but we do have groups that meet like choir . . ." He interrupted again and asked, " Do any of the other churches in town have a singles program?" I said, "I don't think they do, but . . ."

He interrupted again and said, "Well, I appreciate your coming by!" and showed me the door. What a challenge it is to go a second mile with such a person.

What kind of mileage does one get out of this faith on those times and occasions when even pastors must take slow, plodding steps against which the spirit is resistant? Every mile cannot be comfortable and familiar. Some require more. Some have difficult burdens and unreasonable demands. Some push every good intention to the limit. Yet the Christ who beckons and who says, "Follow me!" takes into account the challenge of the extra mile.

To go a little further with someone who is bent on forcing the Christian to demonstrate an unswerving resolve, who is intent on pushing every modest virtue to the breaking point, who is thoughtless and uncaring and only wishes to use another's time or skill or resources, is to know the challenge of the second mile. Life places the Christian in conversations, in relationships, in conditions where every ounce of courage and tolerance and forbearance is tried. Standing in those shoes, advancing in those shoes may require all one has to give. Yet Christ bids those who follow Him to double the official requirement.

Roman law stipulated that unless it was an emergency, no one would be made to go more than one mile. Jewish people often placed pegs in the ground which marked a mile's distance from their houses in every direction. Such was the humiliating experience of legally being forced to be servants that they were as specific as possible about where their duty ended. *(Angel).* "This far and no further," was on the minds and in the hearts of every person made to comply with that law, limiting their capacity beyond it. Jesus opened to them a larger insight and the resources of their faith by instituting the second mile as the more spiritually acceptable distance to go.

A lot of grievances can emerge while traveling the first mile. Resentment, anger, injustice, humiliation may all register themselves. But it is on the second mile that the counterbalances to all of these things are discovered, and one walks lighter and loftier from having found grace and patience and forgiveness and kindness in going the spiritually acceptable distance.

On the spiritual journey, the longest mile is the first mile. One does not travel it voluntarily. One is pressed into service and made to travel farther and longer than is ordinarily required. But there is no taskmaster enforcing such servile duty with a sword or lash. On the spiritual journey, the conscription is self-imposed, and **obedience is what gets exercised.**

What preacher on a circuit has not tinkered with the preaching schedule in order to improve the overall spiritual condition of the charge, or to increase attendance at the church that has the better shot at growth or to make the services more convenient for some who find it difficult to attend at a given time? When I did it and had it approved at a meeting where all the churches were represented, I had no idea of the resistance that was swiftly forthcoming. A few members of one church had their own telephone meeting a day or so later, and it did not take them long to agree that they did not want the change for which they had voted.

In a week's time, I had a door slammed in my face, a cane waved at me by an elderly gentleman, a monthly paycheck withheld and a call from my district superintendent who had heard from the irate and disillusioned members of that small flock. It was a dilemma, but the larger dilemma had to do with my own disillusionment regarding ministry. I could visualize my brief career in ministry suddenly being over! That and other related frustrations and doubts served to place my own inner journey at risk. I wondered if I should just quit.

A conversation with an older minister in a neighboring town opened larger doors for me. He did not sympathize with anything I said. Instead, he made a statement or two which helped me focus on my obedience to God's call. "You are the only pastor they've got," he said. "You've got to love them in all of this. There's nobody else who will do it." I went back home refreshed from that conversation and almost eager to go the next mile with my people.

Left to one's own devices, obedience would never get exercised out on the road. There would be nothing particularly meritorious about one's journey, for it would be no different from any other. How far is one willing to be pressed on the journey to the presence of God? It had better be all the way or else the journey is in jeopardy. To gain all the mileage possible from the Christian faith, one has to follow in blind obedience this provocative directive of Jesus.

Imagine how this crowd of listeners received this spiritual requirement when they heard it from the lips of Jesus. It is reasonable to speculate that such a directive did not set well with them at all. Was He in sympathy with Rome? No, He was in sympathy with putting every person who heard him on the road that led to God through the exercise of their obedience to a lesser authority. This was spiritual practice for those occasions on the road when spirits balk and lives recoil and faithfulness breaks down. This was training for the ultimate hardships one is made to suffer in the service of Christ, and which often demand more than one is willing to give.

On the spiritual journey, the longest mile is the first mile. But it is in that additional length that one must be willing to go that the liberating joys of the road are discovered. The pace is faster, the gait is unencumbered, the stride is rhythmic because a glorious milepost has been reached and passed. Through self-imposed conscription and through the exercise of obedience, one reaches that point on the journey where one chooses to go further, and **the extra distance grants renewal.**

A person who decided to do all in her power to begin a program of physical fitness decided that she would jog. She set her goal for a mile, and every day she would huff and puff in one direction up the road, having to stop and catch her breath long before she could reach her goal. For weeks, she repeated the same routine, but each time, she had to stop and breathe. She had neither the perseverance nor the stamina for the goal, so she decided that she would simply run as far as she could and stop.

There was a bush which marked the place where she would usually stop and bend over and breathe heavily. It was always at that point that she would turn around and walk back home. Gradually, it became the defined limit of her daily jog and, out of habit, she would always stop there and go through a mental and emotional routine of standing there for a little while and winding down.

Imagine the day, months afterward, when a friend of hers met her at her house and jogged with her. When they reached the bush which marked the usual stopping place, both continued on up the road. In a short time they were well beyond the place which roughly served as the designated one mile point. They were well past that when the woman realized that she was not gasping for air but was literally amazing herself with how far they had come. And she kept going.

On the spiritual journey, as the second mile is traveled, the spirit is renewed for the many more miles which are ahead. The extra resources one discovers beyond that point are truly amazing. Stamina, energy, resilience are all joyous and liberating. But none of these are evident until the second mile. From that point, the journey and the person taking it become inseparable, for it has become a choice, a preference, a willingness to claim the great freedom of the road.

Sources:

C. Roy Angel. Iron Shoes. Broadman Press. Nashville, TN. 1953. pp. 94-95.

HELP ALONG THE WAY
Mark 4:35-39

On that day, when evening had come, he said to them, "Let us go across to the other side." And leaving the crowd, they took him with them in the boat, just as he was. And other boats were with him. And a great storm of wind arose, and the waves beat into the boat, so that the boat was already filling. But he was in the stern, asleep on the cushion; and they woke him and said to him, "Teacher, do you not care if we perish?" And he awoke and rebuked the wind, and said to the sea, "Peace! Be Still!" And the wind ceased, and there was a great calm. (Mark 4:35-39)

Few people hitchhike anymore, but occasionally a person will be seen standing out on a long stretch of road with a thumb up, hoping that a car will stop and someone will offer a ride. The odds of that happening are not as good today as they were a few short years ago. Due to the atrocities that have happened to people who have stopped to give strangers a lift, not many will do that now. More often than not, the hitchhiker finds himself walking, sometimes far into the night, because no one is willing to take the risk of being robbed or killed in order to give someone else a ride.

People cannot be blamed for their caution and their attention to common sense, but it remains that there are many people out there who are exposed to the perils of the road because they have unwisely placed themselves in the predicament of seeking assistance from strangers who whiz past them at seventy miles per hour. "That's their problem!" And it is! But even so, it is one more time in somebody's life when an ancient question gets asked: "Doesn't anybody care?"

You and I are going to hear that question a lot in our lives, for we live in a society which has patented phrases like, "That's their problem!" and "I couldn't care less!" Everybody is quick today to expose the false needs of people, to see through the false claims of people, to debunk the so-called misfortunes of people. When is the last time you have heard of anybody having a legitimate need? It is harder and harder to meet legitimate needs in our society, not because more and more people are abusing the system, but because would-be helpers have grown cynnical and genuinely do not care.

In the writing of this sermon, the phone rang no fewer than three times with solicitations for the needs of people. Were they legitimate? Even I myself assume they are not when I say that I do not respond to solicitations over the telephone. Legitimate or phony, by making that response, I have placed myself somewhere in the great living tide of people who shout out with a loud collective voice, "I do not care!" And all the time I perceive myself to be a caring individual.

How should one perceive oneself in a society which speaks such statements in unison? --which rarely finds an occasion anymore to respond out of the goodness of one's heart, which identifies most of the trouble and affliction and desperation and heartbreak in the world with the familiar admonition, "That's their problem!" Such is the social tempest in which we are navigating; such is the perilous public wave we are riding.

"Doesn't anybody care?" That was the question of a local preacher who was trying to get help from his conference Board of Church Development for pews and building repair. "Doesn't anybody care?" This was the question that came from the small church closing its doors because everyone had died. The cry for help is not just being registered by the poor and homeless with their insatiable appetites; it is heard at every level as more and more people are being driven away from the heart and the door and the agency by those who really could not care less!

Environmentalists tell us that wildlife in record numbers have been forced to live in urban and suburban areas because of the encroachment of human progress upon their natural habitats.

Coyotes howl regularly at concerts in Los Angeles's Griffith Park, a mere six miles from city hall, and they have spread across the country to become permanent residents in such cities as Chicago, Cincinnati and Albany. Alligators have wandered onto streets and front lawns in Florida and Louisiana, and foxes have dens in almost every major American city in their climate zone. One was even found under the bleachers in New York City's Yankee Stadium. *(Nyerges).*

If the animals only knew about some of the attitudes and behaviors governing human social systems and the struggle human beings are having living together, they would probably go somewhere else. Perhaps their behavior is a redemptive signal of some kind which says in a very natural way that those who exercise dominion in all of its forms are also expected to care.

For those on the spiritual journey, the care of God for their lives and their futures is what draws them toward God's presence. The journey takes one to the source of love and caring, for it is at this source that all who seek God wish to abide. If God were not loving and caring, no one would want to find the way to His presence. It is the assurance that God knows and cares and loves which makes the journey to God's presence the most important thing about our existence.

One evening when Jesus said to His followers, "Let us go across to the other side," a great storm arose during their journey, and water was filling the boat. The disciples had to wake Jesus, who calmed the wind and the waves; but on waking Him, they said to Him, "Carest thou not that we perish?" or "Do you not care?" What an age old anxiety! What a natural presumption to make, even about the Son of God. "Carest thou not that we perish?" Such a statement is a fresh headline in most human biographies today.

Everyone needs to realize that regardless of how the world is viewed, regardless of how human beings see themselves, regardless of all of the events and activities which happen in the course of life and time, **we are all on a journey to the other side.** Because we are, we have to care and we have to know who else cares. What is the point of any pilgrimage of the heart, any venture of the spirit, if one cannot have the assurance that God cares and loves and holds all of creation precious? Without that great, underlying foundation, nothing has ultimate meaning. The one great hunger that is below the extremities of life, buried deep beneath the rage, lodged far below the brief infrequent joys, is that some great Someone somewhere cares.

The woman on the hospital bed was a member of my church, and she was dying of cancer. She had gone through many emotional upheavals in coming to terms with that great and ultimate fact about herself. Along with her family, I had experienced her anger, her depression, her crying and sorrow. At one point, when we were alone in the room, she confided that she was not ready. "I've believed in God all my life," she said, "but right now, I just don't know! If God is real, and if God loves me, why am I going through this?" My response to her question was totally inadequate. I knew it and she knew it. Yet somewhere in making it, all of my clinical training went out the window in a confessional statement that, when translated, said something like: God knows, God cares, and God sees us safely through to the other side.

The care of God is a prerequisite for the spiritual journey. It is the motivation behind those who seek God's presence. The willingness to forsake houses and lands, to leave mother and father, to go forth in discipleship proclaiming that love and that care, would all be pointless unless God's care were real and attainable. There would be no casting off, no eagerness to get to the other side were it all a hoax or a fantasy or a myth. That God cares is a given or nothing about the journey to His presence makes any sense.

The disciples in the boats felt such assurance, but when the storm arose and the boat filled with water, they began to grow doubtful and desperate about whether they would arrive safely on the other shore. Though Jesus was sleeping calmly and untroubled, they had to wake Him and gain assurance from Him that their faith was not naive. They could not handle the situation without some reassuring word from Him.

We are all on a journey to the other side. **We will meet storms.** They may blow up suddenly and frighten us and fill us with doubts. While our faith may be strong, it always needs the assurance of Christ to fortify it and validate it and give us confidence in God's love and care. In the time of storm and strife, our cry is the cry of those on the boat. "Carest thou not that we perish?" We desperately need to be reassured that whatever befalls us, we are safe and secure in the care of God.

In another generation, it used to be fashionable for couples to go to Niagara Falls on their honeymoon. (My grandparents went there). If you have ever been there, you will recall the cataracts back on the lake which, ultimately, become the falls. If one goes back far enough from the falls, boating can be enjoyed in comparative safety. There is always the slow imperceptible movement of the water, but far enough back one can breast the currents and row a boat.

If, however, the rowing stops and the boat is allowed to drift with that slow steady movement of the waters, danger threatens. If the boat is allowed to drift beyond a certain little island, it is said that no human strength can save it, and it will go plunging over the falls. On one side, safety; on the other, destruction. Someone has named that little island, "Redemption Point." Once beyond, there is no redemption. *(Moore).*

In so many crises of life humanity reaches that emotional dividing line between safety and destruction. So many are poised there, and safety is not always guaranteed. More would perish were not the presence of Christ there with them, but as often is the case, His presence is not enough. The disciples had to rouse Jesus in their boat, and He immediately calmed the winds and the waves. And human beings today, who are in danger of plunging to destruction because they doubt the goodness of God, must rouse the Christ of their faith if they are to be safely kept from harm. On the spiritual journey, one thing is certain and can sustain us. **We have the presence of Christ** to calm our fears and passions and to reassure us that God cares.

My grandparents who went to Niagara Falls are both dead. I miss them, even at the age I am now, because they were so present and so significant in my formative years. One of the great treasures that I own is a taped copy of an old scratched wax phonograph record which they made at some time early in their marriage. Though it is warped and pitted and sounds hopelessly distorted, I can recognize them singing together an old song, "Beyond the Sunset." When I play it, their presence is with me just like it was when I was a child. On the journey, how much more will the presence of Christ touch us and comfort us and assure us that God cares!

"Carest thou not that we perish?" This was the anguished cry of those who roused Jesus from His sleep. But Christ did not come with an explanation; He came with His presence and calmed the wind and the waves. "O yes, He cares; I know He cares; His heart is touched with my grief." The heart of Christ is able to contain the doubts and worries and griefs and distresses of a fearful humanity because it also holds the love of God. The presence of Christ is evidence of God's care in the world. Those on the journey with Him must take note of what that signifies and be encouraged to care for others.

A flight from Denver to Wichita was boarding. On an ambulance litter, an attendant carried a 225 pound man as the last traveler to board. As he was strapped tightly to a seat in the passenger section, it was evident that he was paralyzed from his shoulders down. As the plane taxied to the runway, the force lunged him to the right, causing him to fall toward the next seat. The flight attendant came and propped him up again in an upright position.

Later in the air as food and drinks were served, this man who was about 27 years old could only look as the other passengers were being served food. He was alone with no one to see that his needs were met. After a few moments, another passenger who had noticed, slipped from her seat and inquired if the flight attendant would be helping the man to eat. She said she did not know. The passenger then volunteered to do it. The flight attendant seemed relieved.

The woman passenger introduced herself to the paralyzed man and cut his meal into bite sizes and placed them in his mouth. It was awkward at first, but before long, it became more relaxed and smooth with all the coordination of a natural meal. The young man told her of his unfortunate accident, his lonesomeness, his joys, his struggles, his faith, his hope. His name was Bill. For a short time, their spirits blended, and then the woman returned to her seat. *(Hewett, p. 117).*

So many people need to know that God cares for them. How will they know unless those who follow Christ find time on this journey with Him to be a help along the way.

Sources:

f. Arthur J. Moore. Fight On, Fear Not! Abington Press. Nashville, TN. 1962. p. 112.

James S. Hewett. Illustrations Unlimited. Tyndale House Publishers. Wheaton IL. 1988. p. 117.

Christopher Nyerges in NY Times; quoted in Reader's Digest. nd.

A KNOCK AT MIDNIGHT
Luke 11:5-10

And he said to them, "Which of you who has a friend will go to him at midnight and say to him, 'Friend, hand me three loaves; for a friend of mine has arrived on a journey, and I have nothing to set before him'; and he will answer from within, 'Do not bother me; the door is now shut, and my children are with me in bed; I cannot get up and give you anything'? I tell you, though he will not get up and give him anything because he is his friend, yet because of his importunity he will rise and give him whatever he needs. And I tell you, Ask, and it will be given to you; seek, and you shall find; knock, and it will be opened to you. For everyone who asks receives, and he who seeks finds, and to him who knocks it will be opened. (Luke 11:5-10)

He didn't know me from Adam, yet he left his garage and the car he was working on to come out to take a look at mine. He didn't seem to mind the interruption. "I've never worked on one of these," he said. I could fathom that. It was a foreign car. I had bought it in Atlanta. I was directed to his place out in the county because I had no better option.

"Well, open the hood and let me see it," he said. "The engine is in the back, " I told him. He seemed surprised and said, "I don't reckon so!" When I opened the back and showed him the engine, I could see that he might as well have been gazing upon an alien spacecraft. "It's a leaking fuel injector," I said. "Do you think you can fix it?" He studied it a bit and then said, "Naw, I can't help you." And, without another word, he turned and slowly walked back to his garage.

It was frustrating to stand there and watch him walk off, while getting the unspoken message: "You should have known better than to buy something like that to use out here." Somewhat humiliated at having fallen into the role of the gullible city-slicker, I was about to get back into my car and nurse it home when he stopped, turned around and walked back to me. He said, "But I'll tell you what I will do!" "What is that?" I asked. He put an arm on my shoulder and looked me straight in the eye and said, "I'll sit up all night with you."

How comforting it is, in the middle of strange and untenable situations, to be given some kind of reference point that opens the spiritual door and throws out a mat of acceptance and welcome. How fortifying it is to enter a place or a mood or a moment as a stranger and be recognized and treated as a friend. Who has not been the beneficiary of such generous and hospitable acts on the part of others? In our remembering them and celebrating them as persons who have been dependent and who have been at the mercy of another's good graces, we will know what to do when the knock comes at midnight.

Jesus tells this story to His disciples. A man is awakened in the middle of the night from someone pounding on his door. It is his neighbor who has had an unexpected guest in the middle of the night and who needs to offer his visitor something to eat. He has nothing in the house, so he has come from next door to ask for food. "A friend has arrived on a journey, and I have nothing to set before him!"

Into a well ordered routine, with family fed and put to bed, with the entire community asleep, came a knock at midnight. Interventions will always happen, and when they do, they change the order and the texture of life. They must be accommodated! And often, in the flurry that is stirred by their happening, purposes get realigned or redefined. Nothing is quite as upsetting as a disruptive intervention, but then, nothing is quite as refreshing or as reconstituting.

The unexpected guest used to be a positive image. It brought with it mystery, news, possibility, entertainment, delight. How sad that it has all changed. The unexpected guest today evokes the image of intrusion, interruption, inconvenience, someone being "put upon." It is unthinkable to knock on anyone's door at midnight unless in a dire emergency, and even then, the preference for all involved is 911.

On the spiritual journey, there is a strong temptation to conduct oneself as though it were a solo trip, but there are others on the journey, too. They also look for sustenance and nourishment from time to time, and it is not always convenient to engage them. But if one has the means to provide what is needed, there is little choice but to be inconvenienced and to meet the need that finds its way to one's door. After all, if anyone knocks, should not the expectation be that the door will be opened?

The church in the world has its schedule printed in a weekly bulletin. Everyone can read it and learn of the grace which it alone supplies. But what if the knock comes at midnight when the building is closed and the staff is unavailable and the door is locked and shut? What of those who would inconvenience the peaceful sleep of the church by asking for sustenance and nurture? Would anybody recognize them as members of their own family or as friends? Would anybody go to any length to meet their needs?

What end will one go to in order to help a friend? What must one set before him? The journey is not a solo trip. There are others who are on it, too. To stop and attend to their needs may slow things down, but then again, it may be the beginning of something larger and greater, and it may give dimension and renewal to what has become near-sighted and self-indulgent. Perhaps they arrive at the door in order to make the journey more real to those who are on it but who are lost in themselves.

What end will we go to in order to help a friend? What must we set before those who come to us for nurture and direction? When the knock comes at midnight, **we must help them decide to return to God.** So many who are on this journey have become lost and are crying out to be recognized. When they find their way to us, we must put our spiritual ambitions aside and listen to their broken dreams. We cannot be of genuine assistance to them unless we help them find direction.

On an initial visit to a man and his wife who were members of the church, I rang the doorbell, found no one at home and left a card. The visit was made during my first few weeks in this particular church, and I was attempting to see as many people as possible in order to get names and faces connected and gain some feel for the community. After leaving their door, card stuck in the back door screen, I went on to other homes.

At the end of that particular day, my route carried me back by this same house, and being diligent about my visits, I spied a different car in the yard and decided to stop. As I got out of mine, I noticed that the car in the yard had been recently driven, for those little cooling-off noises were coming from it. Going up to the back screen, I noticed my card was gone. I rapped on the door facing. The back door opened. A woman stood there having just taken off a rather large wig and hooked it over the top of a high-backed kitchen chair. She was also holding a can of beer. All she could say was, "My God!" Recognizing me immediately, she finally regained composure enough to tell me that she never dreamed I would come back after having left my card. That was a visit that made a lasting impression.

There are so many people on so many different roads in life, even in the church. Sometimes they seek us out by knocking on the door of our well-ordered lives to ask us if we recognize them. Sometimes we are the ones who do the knocking, and these same issues of recognition and direction are almost immediately raised. Behind all of the facades and the roles of who they are and who we are, behind all of the wigs and the calling cards, can we identify them as friends who have specific needs that are ours to address? To what length will we go to engage them and enjoy them and to help them reconnect with God?

"A friend has come on a journey and I have nothing to set before him!" Too often this has been the reality of those times and occasions when genuine need arrives on the doorstep of the Christian witness and the Christian Church. What length will anyone go to in order to recognize, identify and redirect those who wander on the spiritual road? The meaning of a friend is one who will love at all times; who, knowing all of the disappointing things about a person, will still continue to accept that person and be a friend.

What end will we go to in order to help a friend? What must we set before those who come to us for help? When the knock comes at midnight, **we must help them renew their vows.** Not everyone keeps the commitments that were once made with gladness and resolve. People fail! People falter! People fall by the way! Often they go unrecognized by the Christian community and there is nothing to remind them of their vows. When they knock at midnight, they are knocking for a reason. They knock at our particular door because they are reminded of Christ.

One night in the seventies, about midnight, I was working in the office at the church. It was winter, and it was raining outside. From my window, I could see the lighted street, and I noticed three people in white robes making their way to my door after having seen my light on the inside. They were thoroughly soaked. I went out into the hallway and opened the door, and there stood three young Hare Krishnas, two young men and a young woman, smiling at me and shivering. One of them did all the talking. "Brother," he said, "I wonder if you would be kind enough to let us come in from the cold and get warm and dry?"

Apprehensive about the hour of the night, I hesitated. Then I let them in. The next question was, "Brother, I wonder if you would allow us to stay inside here for the rest of the night. It is only for a few hours." I ended up showing them a heated room in the building where they could finish out the evening. In the course of our conversation, I found out that these were kids from Georgia who had grown up in the Christian Church. The one doing the talking was very zealous about his Vedic beliefs. The other two did not look as if they thought it was the best way to spend an evening.

The next morning, I treated these three to breakfast. All heads turned and conversation stopped at a local cafe where they were served eggs and bacon, piping hot. The spokesman said, "I'm sorry, brother, but we aren't allowed to eat this food." The lady who owned the establishment was a friend of mine. And she happened to hear what the young man said. Her words to him were harsh. "Buddy, if you can't eat my cooking, you can leave." And then she whispered to me, "If you don't get these people out of here, I'm calling the law."

The leader of the group got up to leave, still smiling. One of his young friends got up with him, ready to go. The young woman looked at him and said, "I'm eating it. I'm starving!" I sat there with her while she wolfed down two of the three plates of food after the others had made their exit. I said, "Aren't you going with your friends?" She then poured out her story of how she missed her home and her parents and the life she had given up. "Just spending the night in a church reminded me of how much I have missed mine. It's been almost a year since I've seen my mother and dad!"

We talked on for a while, and the upshot was that I called her father who asked me to help her get a bus ticket. By midmorning, she was on her way back to a life she had forsaken and to parents who had no idea where she had been and who had grieved their loss each day. Unwittingly, I had participated in a parable of Jesus, though it did not register with me until years later!

The spiritual journey is not a solo trip. Others are on it, too. Sometimes they need us to help them decide to return to God; sometimes they need us to help them renew their vows. If we are resourceful in helping them when they knock on the door of our lives, we find validation for ourselves and a refreshment and refocus that makes the journey more compelling. In reminding them of Christ, we also remind ourselves, and it calls to mind that saying of His, "There is no greater love than to lay down one's life for one's friend."

What length will you and I go to in order to help a friend? What must we set before our friends in order to be of help to them? When the knock comes at midnight, it is not enough to offer an explanation or good advice. **We must offer ourselves for use.**

When Jesus told this story to His disciples, He described the man seeking food for a friend as one who did not have resources but who knew where to get them. Even though he had to dress and go out and wake up another, even though he had to strain a relationship, even though it made him highly uncomfortable to do it, he did what it took to get the loaves.

Sometimes the cost is discomfort, humiliation, refusal and rejection in order to do what it takes to recognize and accommodate and feed those who turn to us as they look for help and direction. Unless there is a willingness to give them our time, our interest, our consideration, our love, anything else we give them will not be of any real assistance. Christ made an offering of Himself for the sins of the whole world. You and I must offer ourselves to those who need us to remind them of Christ.

There is a man in my church who is quiet and unassuming. He does many of the little thankless jobs there are to do around a church, yet he is so unobtrusive that he is barely noticed. He opens and shuts certain doors, picks up the litter, gets the lights, takes the bulletins to the sanctuary. If they need folding or stuffed with an insert, he handles the job. Aside from these regular things, he is the one who helps with the Christmas tree. He is the one who helps carry things in and out. If something needs to be taken home and mended, this man does it without asking anyone and without telling anyone. If someone asks him to help out, even to the point of personal inconvenience, he is always gracious, always willing to be of assistance. He never shows he is bothered by any of it, even when he is put upon.

One thing about Bill . . . When he isn't there, everyone notices! A lot of things simply do not get done. Yet no one has ever suggested that he be thanked publicly or that he be honored for all that he does. It would almost seem to be inappropriate to focus that kind of attention upon him. Rather than appreciate it, accolades would be an embarrassment to him. Recognize him for anything and one would almost take away the aura that is so self-defining. As it is now, Bill serves a larger function than being the doer of a long list of deeds. He is the unofficial hand of welcome to anyone and everyone who seems misplaced or uncomfortable. If it is a visitor who doesn't know his way around or a transient looking for a meal, Bill is the one who makes her feel at home, who shows him to a room or who invites him inside. He reminds everybody of Jesus Christ.

To what inconvenience will we go in order to remind people of Christ? What will it take for us to treat it as an opportunity rather than an inconvenience? When the knock comes at midnight, and it always does, there are many options. One is to pretend not to hear it and go back to sleep. Another is to become angry and grudge those who are making the disturbance. But the Christ who is the open door would have all who follow Him open the door at once and extend the gracious invitation to come inside.

THE GATHERING LIGHT
John 8:12

Again Jesus spoke to them, saying, "I am the light of the world; he who follows me will not walk in darkness, but will have the light of life." (John 8:12)

Running alone in the dark before the sun comes up, before the car engines start and traffic is a din on the far-off highway, one can find time to think. Birds have not waked, wind has not picked up; the day has not begun to stir. The only sounds are the solitary tapping of one's feet on the pavement and the paced breathing that is always the same. Occasional street lights are still on, but one is mainly in the dark between them, looking far away to the next, lost in preoccupation as the quiet grants time for snatches of solitude which are surprisingly thorough and long.

Then dawn comes on the road, simply, gradually, like the patient lifting of a dark veil. It comes in faded echelons of light. Stars wink out. The first birds stir themselves and sing. Squirrels move on the bark of the pines as they sense the morning approaching. There is twilight imagery. On the pavement, one looks at a small limb or is it a snake? Motors bark, doors bang, the street lights go out one by one as things emerge from their shadows and are touched by brightness.

And then suddenly the day actually breaks, though no sun has come over the horizon. Clouds are pink and the sky appears larger. Insects begin their whirring. Birds sing out over their territories. Movement and a faint mist are apparent as the one who runs beats it back to his own driveway before the heat of the sun can be felt upon his back, having gone through all of the changes that move the world from night to day.

The great thing about the spiritual journey is that time when dawn comes on that particular road. Perhaps the way has been silent and solitary and the follower of Christ has groped in the darkness part of the way. But as the sky begins to brighten and the light gradually comes, that road becomes less ominous and more inviting, less isolated and more interesting, less reflective and more active. The spiritual journey constitutes a movement that is progressive, just like dawn on the road. And the amazing thing about it has do to with what gets caught and identified in the gathering light.

Jesus made many startling statements about Himself. One of them, which He made to the scribes and Pharisees, was perhaps the most startling of all. "I am the light of the world," He said. "Whoever follows me will not walk in darkness, but will have the light of life." This is the promise Christ makes to those who follow Him on the spiritual journey. They will not have to fear the darkness of the road. To follow Christ is like watching the sun come up on the road. He is the light of the world, and those who journey in His name are caught and drawn toward Him in his gathering light.

Moths are creatures who generally find their way around by following the light of the moon. Unfortunately, moths cannot tell the difference between the moon and other lights; that is why they are so vulnerable at night. If a light is turned on and a moth sees it, the moth will start circling it. It will fly around a light bulb until it becomes disoriented and temporarily loses its sense of direction. Moths cannot tell one light source from another, and often they are destroyed because they fly right into the wrong light source which is often the head lamp of a moving automobile.

Those whom Christ would gather on the road to follow after Him are drawn by His spiritual presence. And it is truly the light of the world. Those who come after Him can identify Christ from every other light source and follow where He leads. Whatever darkness one encounters will only be temporary, for He has promised never to leave anyone alone without the light of His presence. On the spiritual journey, we are never without the confidence that there is more light up ahead.

This journey constitutes a movement that is progressive, and the first movement is to **meditation.** When one is quiet and still, it is easier to collect one's thoughts and to meditate uninterrupted. A lot of people walk and run early in the mornings because this is their reflection time or their prayer time. You see people at all hours of the day with their headsets on, but those who elect to go while it is dark, before the dawn, usually enjoy the quiet of their surroundings. The movement from darkness to light is progressive, and the first movement is generally the meditative one.

One of my best memories of the church of my childhood was of the night when the lights went out in the middle of the evening service. The preacher's name was T.D. George. He was an elderly gentleman who wore glasses. Brother George used a manuscript in his preaching, and when the lightning cracked and the thunder boomed and the church was left in pitch dark, he could not continue. An usher immediately brought one of the altar candles up to the pulpit, but the light wasn't good enough for Brother George to resume where he had left off. He proceeded with, "We'll just all sit quietly until the lights come back on."

Well, they never did. And the small group who attended sat there in a darkened building watching his dim image in the candlelight and listening to the pops and noises of the building. The longer everyone sat there, the more important the evening became. The transitions which occurred in those moments were awe-inspiring. Someone in front of me barely could be heard whispering a prayer. It was like sitting in the same room with God and talking with Him. Later when the ushers used the candles to show everyone the way out, no one showed any enthusiasm over having to leave. In our church, the night in the dark without the sermon was a progressive step.

On the spiritual journey, following in the steps of Christ, one takes progressive steps. The first ones are generally meditative. In the early darkness before being drawn toward the light, one has time to think and meditate. It is a necessary part of the solitude of that road. One is wise to use such time to humble oneself, to open one's life and contemplate the needs, desires and goals that often have not been carefully thought through. When it is too dark for anything else, one has time and occasion to think. And no journey should be taken without considerable thought as to why one continues to follow Christ, how far one has come, how much further one has to go. As one journeys toward the light of Christ, the darkness right before the dawn of insight and revelation is meditative for a time, and then there is a second movement. One goes from meditation to **inspiration.**

Out on the road where I live, as soon as that brightness comes with the dawn and things gradually emerge from the shadows, the lake behind the houses comes alive with the quacking and honking of ducks and geese, as they flutter about and beat their wings and prepare to launch themselves toward the breaking of the day. At first there is a great flurry as the geese honk and leave the water in a group. They are invisible, but one can hear their wings whistle and their honking increase as they make a slow circle to gain height and momentum. If one pauses and follows the sounds, eventually their silhouettes can be seen as they rise above the still-dark landscape and head for different waters. It is an inspiring sight.

For the faithful traveler on the spiritual journey, the progress on that particular road is from meditation to inspiration as light of Christ becomes more apparent. While things are not distinctly clear and visible, there is the promise that they will be. The heart is stirred; the step is quickened; the mind is alert to a world that is rapidly unfolding. It is a time, not for meditation or quiet reflection, but for connection with all that one knows about Christ —the stories of His ministry, the miracles of His healing, the words of life that are remembered and known by heart. As things pick up and brighten and the road becomes more illuminated, one becomes inspired by the life of Christ.

In my early years of ministry, I took part in the service for a man who was late for his own funeral. The church was out in the country. The hearse had a flat tire on the way. It took time to get the casket in the back of a borrowed pick-up and to the church. To make matters worse, I had assumed that I was assisting, so I had no prepared remarks. The town minister who was my elder assumed that he would be assisting, since the person had technically been on the roll of one of the churches I pastored. Realizing this multiplicity of errors, he told me not to worry.

When the service got underway, I read the 23rd Psalm and had a prayer. My senior brother then rose without a note and commenced, "We have here before us a man's man! He walked like a man! He talked like a man! He smelled like a man . . ." And on and on he went, drawing from the great reserves within himself. Everyone forgot about the delay. They were drawn and riveted to this man's eloquent as well as earthy remarks. The family sobbed in the pew. The crowd was mesmerized. They were all inspired.

Those who would follow Christ cannot do so from the classic, static postures. There has to be movement. There has to be inspiration and faith to journey toward His light. "I am the light of the world," He said. "Whoever follows me will not walk in darkness." But so many who claim to follow have never moved beyond the meditative state. With His dawn upon the road, there must be a progressive movement. One goes from meditation to inspiration, and then there is the third movement. One goes from inspiration to **motivation.**

Once there were three priests, a Dominican, a Franciscan and a Jesuit, who were visiting a shrine. Suddenly the lights went out. It was so dark that one could not see his hand in front of his face. The Dominican priest stood up in the darkness and said, "Let us consider the nature of light and darkness, their meaning, and how each is a gift from God for the benefit of human kind." The Franciscan began to sing a hymn of praise to "Our Little Sister Darkness." The Jesuit went out and replaced the burned out fuse.

Meditation is such a necessary part of the Christian faith. It gives focus, centering, an ability to discern the great issues of life. And inspiration is a vital part. There are great moments, great realizations, great times of insight which need to be highlighted and illuminated. But the critical thing needed in the Christian faith is motivation, that which prompts one from the inner disciplines to the outer expressions and takes one out of the sanctuary and out onto the road that leads to life.

There are a lot of casualties on the highways and roads of this country, small game that never makes it out of the way of a speeding automobile, birds that fly up and bounce off windshields, pets that wander across at the wrong time. A lot of animals lose their lives because they allow distractions to place them in harm's way, especially those who are nocturnal and who are blinded and paralyzed by light.

There are spiritual casualties on the journey to God. Many of them never leave the quiet of the sanctuary; many of them never get beyond meditation and prayer; many of them are paralyzed by light, never having known what it means to risk the high adventure of the road. As His dawn gradually comes, Christ beckons all who follow to move forward toward the light of His life. As it is made plainer to everyone, as it illuminates more fully the road ahead, those walking in that direction are motivated to be all they can in His name and in His power.

Speaking of casualties on the highways, there is a little town in South Georgia which is the proverbial "hole in the road." It consists of a crossroads with a blinker light. Yet at each right-hand lane of the intersection, there are huge metal "walk / don't walk" posts which appear over-compensating and ridiculous.

Stopping there for gas, I asked an old man whose idea this had been. He said that some larger town had bought new ones and had given these old ones to their little town. "But they don't work," he said! I remarked that it seemed like an awfully useless gift. He said, "It doesn't matter. No one ever crosses the road here."

If the Christian faith is going to make the difference in the future that it has in the past, something is going to have to motivate believers out of their dysfunctional postures at all the sleepy crossroads and move them to the high road of adventure in the name of Christ. Perhaps in the movement from a believer to a follower, one also moves from being a casualty to becoming an active participant. Nothing motivates the believer any more than the Christ who invites him to be a follower.

"I am the light of the world," He said! Believing that, how can one abide in the shadows and the stillness and never take those progressive steps which reveal the faith more fully. Believing that, how can one choose not to go and be part of the spiritual force that would take all with it to the presence of God; believing that, how can one exhibit caution and reserve and fearfulness when there is one ahead who promises always to light the way. If one dares to be a follower, one must journey toward the light.

It was the last night of revival. The preacher was a dud. People had continued to come out of loyalty and respect for their church and not because of any great or inspiring message. The services had been worse than "ho-hum." The preacher had such a struggle getting some of his words out, those in the pew appeared to be pained, as if they wished to help him. Finally, the torture was brought to a close with the altar call and the last hymn. Everybody was miserable and glad for it to be over, including the one who had struggled to bring the message.

Then a young woman stepped out with a smile on her face, came up and shook the preacher's hand during the second verse of, "Just As I Am," and then turned and faced the congregation. The look on her face must have urged someone to join her, because another young woman stepped out, joined hands with her and continued singing. Then one by one, the entire group got up and joined hands and sang from the front of the altar rail. When the song ended, the piano started up again and everyone joined in to sing, "I Am Thine, O Lord." Every person in the building felt a special touch that evening because that young woman stepped out. And later that night, the talk was not about how badly the preacher had done but about how the church had been revived. God's Spirit had moved each person from being a believer to being a follower.

Sometimes progress on the spiritual journey is only made in increments, like dawn on the road. It begins perhaps as an ominous journey, filled with so many individual difficulties, but as the way is made more plain, as more of its features are revealed, the difficulties eventually vanish and become inconsequential in the movement from darkness to light. Those who are on that road should always be of good cheer. Christ has gone ahead to light the way.

THE CHRIST OF THE CROSSROADS
John 14:18

"I will not leave you comfortless; I will come to you." (John 14:18)

The letter came folded inside a greeting card a few days before Christmas. It was unusual to begin with because this was the first time a letter had ever been included with the customary signed card; but, most of all, it was unusual because he had written it, and he was never much to write anybody. After a few awkward lines, wishing happiness for the holidays, he wrote these words:
"Margaret and I just don't understand it. It's been almost two years now, and our son doesn't even know we are alive. We always felt we did our best with Frank, bringing him up in the church and getting him through college. You remember that time he rebelled against everything. He had us worried for awhile. When he met Fran, we were happy because she was a deeply religious person. It looked like things would turn out right after all, but shortly after they married, they got involved in this new church. Then things just seemed to go wrong.
"When Frank came home, all he could talk about was that church of his. Nothing else could be mentioned without him getting back to that one subject. His mother and I were concerned about it and said as much. Frank really blew his top, and we haven't seen him since. We tried calling, but neither of them will talk to us. It almost broke Margaret's heart, and it has really been hard for us this week.

"A few months ago, we heard that something happened in their church, and they both quit. We have called them and called them, but they still refuse to talk to us. I am worried about Frank. I am afraid he doesn't believe anything. You were close to him when you were here. Is there some way you can help us?"

This request represents one leaf in a bulging portfolio of Christian concerns that should have top priority. Far from being an isolated incident, it is the stereotype in a society already bent out of shape by its pursuit of happiness and identity and meaning. Change the name and alter the circumstances slightly, and it fits a staggering majority of individuals caught in the equivalent of a spiritual nightmare. How does it happen? Somewhere on the journey their simple faith runs the gantlet in a confused and complicated world and is dealt a staggering blow.

What happens to the lives which emerge as emotional and mental embarrassments to those who live them? What happens to the spirits so distraught that they are driven to desert what they are called to become in Jesus Christ? Like puzzles with the pieces missing, many who have earnestly sought the Kingdom of God have found a half-life rather than a new life. They are caught at the crossroads, and they are unable to decide.

The journeys of some are plagued with anguish and confusion. On the way to the presence of God, many a hearty traveler is confronted with bewildering experiences which undermine the affirmations he made at the beginning. Alternatives work their will in the mind and heart. Ideals are abandoned. Exceptions to the rules diffuse the rules themselves. The great mission one visualizes cannot be accomplished for the deviations from it which ultimately obscure it completely.

One of the distinguishing features of the space program has been the excellent communication that has gone on between the astronauts and the ground controllers. Though trained and groomed for years to do a job which consists of memorizing hundreds of procedures, the astronauts are acquainted with numerous variations in each procedure which can, at any time, affect the success of the mission. Communication with the ground controllers has often resulted in course corrections which could not have been determined by the astronauts themselves.

It is the same with the spiritual journey. Without the counsel and guidance of someone who is thoroughly familiar with the variables and who can offer course corrections, its future is in doubt. The spiritual journey is predicated upon a Christ acquainted with all the choices and who stands ready to recommend the right one.

Before He departed from them, Jesus assured those who followed Him that He would not forsake them. They had walked many roads together, but now His was taking Him elsewhere. So that they might not lose heart and become discouraged, He promised to greet them at every crossroads and make the way plain for them. "I will not leave you comfortless," he said. "I will come to you."

Jesus Christ is the faithful guide. He understands the desolation in a life that is unsure of which direction to take. He cares about those who cannot decide. That is why He stands at every crossroads of faith, ready to help those who must choose between opposing directions.

Some years ago, the craze was a Rubik's Cube. If you were one of the lucky ones who could work it, you know that it had nothing to do with luck. There were only two ways to work this six-sided block of frustration so that it would come out with the one arrangement you were looking for out of 43 quintillion possibilities. The first way was to read a book on how to solve it and follow it step by step. But the best way was to hand the cube to someone who knew how it was done, and learn from that person. *(f. McFarland, p. 3).*

You and I can read the Bible for life's solutions, but Jesus Christ is the problem solver in a world where the problems are compounded daily. When one pushes for those encounters with Him, solutions emerge which make the path plainer and the way straighter. Those who seek the right road must first find the Christ who can guide them to it. His comfort and assurance are essential to those who have lost confidence in their ability to continue.

His leadership is a great relief to those so frustrated they would gladly follow. Jesus Christ is the one who can provide a fresh start on the same journey when it stalls at the dividing of the road.

Every journey of the spirit that begins with good intentions must come at length to a crossroads that prevents any further progress. One such spiritual crossroads is **temptation,** where good intentions are usurped by greater persuasions and faith falls under siege.

Ours is the age of impulse. One thinks, speaks and acts on the basis of those urgent demands each situation calls for, choosing from an assortment of values those particular ones which solicit popularity and approval and whatever else is promised at the moment. Life is always a case of "here and now!" "Do it!" "Go for it!" —without caution and without conscience. One selects from it as from a Whitman's Sampler, and that which is the most tempting usually dictates the choice.

A man came back to church after some years as an inactive member. He was amazed at the difference made in his life when he allowed himself to be influenced more by church friends than by secular friends. He said one day in a Sunday School class: "I don't think it is morally wrong to take a drink now and then, and I had been in the habit of doing so every night before going to bed. I still don't think it is wrong, but since I've been coming back to church, I don't feel the need to do it any more."

Good company imparts good influence. To be in Christ is to be in good company. Christ reminds people of who they are by reminding them of who He is! He is able to rouse the spirit to its former state of vigilance and point it once again to the road He walks. It is He who stands at the crossroads of temptation to redirect those who would turn aside.

The greatest danger awaiting those who are on the spiritual journey is in losing the desire to continue once the novelty of it has passed. Somewhere enroute to the presence of God, conditions are not as fresh or as fascinating as they were at the outset. Privations and inconveniences make the progress difficult. Just when one successfully traverses one crossroads of the spirit, another one appears. To have resisted temptation is nothing when compared with fighting to keep one's strength. A second spiritual crossroads is **weakness,** where endurance and stamina are severely tested and perseverance is doubtful. Luxury and affluence have a way of defeating discipline and resourcefulness. American society is characterized by those who lack self-control, who cave in to a habit, who possess no will power. A battle is being fought on every level to retain strength and to overcome weakness, but few win the battle by themselves.

One of the reasons spas and health clubs have become so popular is the peer reinforcement which stimulates individuals to "hang in there" until they win their battle with the bulge. A person who is overweight may have little motivation to "go it alone," especially when there has been a poor track record of sticking to a diet or to an exercise program. Miserable with themselves, many will admit defeat because they feel they cannot do it on their own. Put them in a group exercise program and they become winners. They work out with zeal and enthusiasm because there are others who fortify them and who, through identification with their issues, give them resolve and strength.

In the face of weakness, few are able to muster the strength to continue on. Exhaustion, disappointment, cowardice and a host of other reasons convince them that the strength simply isn't there for future endeavors. That is why Christ stands at the crossroads, willing to add His strength to those who are weak.

"I will not leave you comfortless," Jesus said. "I will come to you!" Though His presence does bring comfort and strength at all times and in all places, it is never more available to the average wayfarer than it is at the crossroads. It gives direction to the tempted; it gives help to the weak; yet never is it more powerful than when it gives meaning to those who no longer believe. A third spiritual crossroads is **disenchantment,** the one most difficult to walk away from.

More mental illness is couched in religious terms than is defined under any other terminology. More emotional anguish is the result of spiritual struggle than any other single factor. For every person led to Christ each day, multitudes are misled. At the crossroads of disenchantment, one has to stand in line and wait his turn, for a crowd surrounds it and more are coming.

There is devastation in the life which cries out, "I am a failure! I can't see any results! I don't know what to believe! I've lost faith in everything!" The unswerving loyalty, the total dedication, the blind devotion so characteristic of the neophyte are dashed to pieces by some traumatic experience, and the result is hopelessness or hostility or a rejection of that which has been most precious. Disenchantment is where great plans end and disillusionment begins.

Everywhere one looks, people have given up. And they have given up on everything. One hears of people who say they have given up on America, denouncing its leaders and its corrupt system, believing and networking the absolute worst about it. Stand those same people in a crowd before a flag with a crisp breeze blowing and a band playing the "Star-Spangled Banner," and what happens to them is truly amazing. At first, they do not say anything, but as they notice others around them singing, they are usually stirred to the point where they participate, and somewhere during the singing of the tune, they develop the capacity to affirm the best about their country and themselves.

It is in this same spirit that Jesus Christ greets those who are disenchanted and excites them out of their hopelessness. He stands ready to affirm the best in those who believe the worst and to help them turn the corner on their failure and disillusionment. He can be found at every crossroads of faith, pointing people in the right direction.

A young man who entered the ministry with deep convictions and shining expectations suddenly found himself leaving the ministry because of difficulties which arose in the church he served. Heartbroken and spiritless from the shock of this unforeseen reversal in his life, he knew despair as few others have known it. Eventually picking up the threads of a shredded career, he entered the business world, and in a brief time, made a place for himself in it. The advancements, when they came, were well-deserved, but they never released him from the disappointment and the humiliation and the failure of that earlier experience. The outer life had moved out into the mainstream of the traffic while the inner life had stalled at the intersection.

A few years later something happened. This man re-entered the ministry, but not without a great deal of sober assessment. He was older and considerably more realistic than the young man who ventured forth so optimistically years before, but he was remarkably equal to the task. He stood for a long time at the crossroads, but he finally encountered the Christ who was also there.

Every journey must be taken with some degree of risk, but on those journeys of the spirit, one must risk everything. There will be times of exultation, but there will also be occasions when fragile hopes are placed in jeopardy, when ideals must run against the barricades, when worthy ambitions have to be abandoned, and dreams with them. Every road has its treacherous places, but it is at the crossroads where the way cannot be decided that the waiting Christ appears, ready to embrace with open arms.

Sources:

Ken McFarland. Solving Hopeless Problems. in Signs of the Times. Feb. 1982, p. 3.

FRESH PERSPECTIVES
John 12:19

The Pharisees then said to one another, "You see that you can do nothing; the world has gone after him. (John 12:19)

A young man named Phil lived about as orderly and as boring a life as humanly possible. One could set a watch by him. He would come to work at the same time every morning, sit at a desk until his lunch hour. Then he would take his bag with a sandwich in it and go to the vending area, buy a canned drink from the machine and sit there eating until time to return for the second half of the workday at the desk. Phil was a good employee, quiet, nondescript, always on time. To others who worked nearby, he might as well have been a piece of furniture.

Once away from the workplace, on an average day of the week, things would not pick up very much. Phil would go home, feed his cat and pet her a little, open a can of something for supper and eat his meal while he watched the evening news. After that, he would clean up, tend to the same set of eternal chores, read the paper, call his mother on the phone, and then go to bed and read. And this was pretty much the drill for Phil. It was as methodical and as predictable as a late Saturday night re-run.

All of this would change on Friday nights. On Friday nights, Phil's routine would go out the window. If someone who worked with him or who lived in his neighborhood could see him in action out on the dance floor, lost in a crowd of people twisting to country music, no one would have believed that it was Phil. Left to himself, in the monotony of his daily routine, Phil was nothing to write home about. But let loose in a crowd, especially on a dance floor, Phil would suddenly be transformed into a party animal.

Some people find their niche or their identity in a larger way when they are in a crowd. However they happen to be personally, the crowd mentality creates an altogether different dynamic. History has generally profiled the crowd mentality in a negative way in benchmark literary pieces like *The Ox-Bow Incident*, or in political movements like the Nazism of the 1930's, but crowds can lend a positive attitude to some people. The negative features are around today in places like the Middle East where crowds come together for protest or mourning. Yet the positive is more often displayed in all sorts of gatherings such as sports events or concerts or lines of people waiting to gain an autograph.

Crowd mentality gives some people a special sense of belonging that they do not experience individually. The power of this kind of group participation energizes them and brings out in them attributes and behaviors rarely displayed on the personal level. One might think that she knows herself, or one might believe himself incapable of changing a belief or a view; but the lives of people can manifest themselves quite differently when they are played to a crowd.

Jesus found this to be the case with His own life. When viewed from the common perspective of one-on-one with those whom He touched and taught and befriended, the respect and trust and intimacy in His relationships defined Him very naturally as a personal Lord and Savior. But when He had to cope and contend with great crowds of people, that dynamic changed and persons experienced an expanded version of who He was. Because of the crowds who came to hear Him, some larger part of Him emerged in an energy of its own. And those who stood by, who watched in skepticism, were forced to consider Him from a new perspective.

A Southern phenomenon that people run across occasionally is the practice of "stepping on a lost weed." I learned about this unusual occurrence from an elderly woman in a grocery store out in the country as I was making my exit with my bread and milk. I heard the term as it was spoken to someone else and inquired. The woman said, "Oh, you know what it means! If you are out walking in the woods and come upon something familiar from a different angle and don't recognize it at first, or when you are driving somewhere and nothing you see makes any kind of sense, and you swear you are going one way when you are really going the other. When things like this happen and you lose your sense of direction, that means you've done stepped on a lost weed."

Some of the people who experienced the great transition when their perspective on Jesus shifted from an individual to an icon probably felt like they had stepped on a lost weed. He was the same person they had always known, yet when placed in the chemistry of a crowd, it was like seeing Him for the first time. Their recognition of Him had to give way to a different perspective.

Picture the great crowds who followed Jesus from place to place, listening to Him, calling out His name, pressing against Him. Many of them left what they were doing on the day when He was in the vicinity and spent the day with Him. Why? What compelled the crowds to follow, or what compelled people to come together and form a crowd in the first place? Could it be that they were responding to the universality of His message and His ministry which transcended the value of who He was on a personal level? Possibly! Could it be that in this arena, one was more apt to engage the symbolic in such encounters with Him? Also possible! But suppose that what compelled the crowds to be drawn to Him was something more fundamental and practical and less high-flown. Suppose it was just that Jesus saw life clearly, and He revealed it to them.

Not many people like January and February because it is usually cold, it rains, and things appear bleak and drab. I happen to like these months because they seem clean and precise. You and I can see at greater distances because the foliage is gone and the colors are muted, and we can spot birds and animals and other objects which are incredibly far removed from us. Things are "bare bones" and in the stark realities of what they are. There is something very honest about these dormant months when, on clear, crisp days, the sky is at its bluest. While it is nice to see flowers bloom and grass grow and life come out of its shell, things can somehow be seen more clearly and for what they are during the winter months. Faith, too, must take into account the stark realities and have a clear view of God's love and life's limits. No person has ever been more honest and more direct about issues of life and faith than Jesus. That is why crowds were drawn to Him. That is why people were compelled to come.

All kinds of people sought out Jesus because He saw life clearly, and His teaching and preaching revealed it to those who came and listened and understood. And they were not only those of His religion and His race. Such was the clarity of His words and His life that all varieties of people sought Him out. There were even some Greek people who came looking for this Jew, saying, "We would see Jesus!" *(John 12:21)*.

This phenomenon with the crowd disturbed the Pharisees. They did not mind it when only His disciples tagged along. But when He began to draw great and overflowing crowds, when He had to separate himself from them by standing in a boat or on the top of a hill, they knew that something larger than occasional teaching was going on. "Look," they said when they saw the crowds, "the whole world has gone after him!"

When Jesus, the personal Lord and Savior, the guide and companion on the spiritual journey, is placed within the context of the crowd, He must be considered from a fresh perspective. No longer just the archetypal solitary figure who walks the long miles of the winding road, this same Jesus must be contemplated differently. No longer a private version of one's quest for the Kingdom of God, this same Jesus must be viewed and understood as also the catalyst of a group dynamic, something close to the religious imagery of being the Head of the Church.

This journey of the spirit to the presence of God is not solely an individual exercise. What must also get exercised, if one is to experience it in the fullness of its power, is the group dynamic, the crowd mentality as it also seeks a corporate life in Him. To come to know the Christ of the road is to have this fresh perspective of who He is. No longer personal in His entirety. For once the Pharisees had it right! The whole world has gone after Him.

In His speaking to the crowds, Jesus saw life clearly and gave fresh perspectives on what He saw. After listening to Him, **they admitted that they did not have forever.** Remember the crowd who saw Him raise Lazarus from the dead? That was a crowd event, not just a private family gathering. Jesus meant it to be so. In taking them from sorrow and doubt and pessimism to joy and hope beyond the grave, Jesus knew that the crowd was privately playing over its own mortality in that exercise. No one went away from there jumping for joy. Every person had been confronted with his own mortality, with how fragile and fleeting her own life was. Certainly, He instilled in them all the hope of the resurrection, but they also had to consider the spectre of death. It was a psychically traumatic episode which Jesus also used as a teaching tool to transform the spiritual apathy of the crowd.

Those who understand themselves to be on the road with Christ, following in His steps in the direction that leads to God, must not style themselves to go blindly with Him, one on one. There are dimensions of their Lord and Savior which are larger and more expanded than their personal spiritual version. The Pharisees were quick to catch on when they noticed that His life not only attracted a few disciples but also large crowds and even those of other nationalities. In a glance, they who had been blind to Him finally saw what they did not want to accept. This wasn't just a leader of individuals who was walking one of the paths leading to the well. Everyone was paying attention. Everyone was listening! Even they were! The whole world was going after Him!

Such was this engaging nature, this catalytic capacity of Jesus that He drew and held great crowds, instructing them and convincing them with His words of life. He saw life clearly, and He gave them fresh perspectives on what He saw. On listening to Him, **they took seriously his power.** Remember the crowd who watched Him divide the loaves? This was a crowd event, not just the handling of an emergency. Jesus meant it to be so. Before initiating this great miracle of loaves and fish, Jesus had the crowd first sit down and be attentive. And there, before God and before them, He blessed and broke insignificant amounts belonging to a youngster and distributed them as a priest would distribute a sacrament, saying things like, "Let this child's gift feed you and show you how to treat one another." And one is led to believe that those in the crowd took their cue and participated in a miracle by which five thousand were fed. Jesus used this experience as a teaching tool to transform the selfish behavior of a crowd.

When Jesus is pictured as the solitary guide on the spiritual road, it is a natural and almost nostalgic portrayal of who He authentically is. But place Him in a crowd, and one is forced to have a fresh perspective that expands His presence beyond the role of personal coach or mentor. To miss this feature of His person is to restrict one's understanding of His power. Part of the journey for every person is to also interface with the crowd event for the purpose of witnessing this aspect of His person. Miss that, and one misses the larger understanding of who Christ is and the larger lessons that He came to teach.

There were always crowds who came to hear Jesus. They sought Him out because He saw life clearly, and He could give them fresh perspectives on what He saw. When they were attentive to Him, **they saw the world through His eyes.** Remember the crowd that lined the streets when he entered Jerusalem? That was the largest crowd of all. Jesus played upon all the symbols that day. It was the day of the new spiritual rule. It was the day of public statement in the temple. It was the day when people saw through the trappings of who they were and dealt with the sin that ran to the core of all their little systems. They saw the world through His eyes, and even as they stood there wondering and waving, they did not like what they saw.

They knew what was coming, just as He knew. None of them wanted to see what He showed them, but they were powerless to shut it out of their minds. Jesus used the events of the day as teaching tools to acquaint all of them with the extensiveness of their acceptable and comfortable sins. Only in a crowd could He have so totally and so thoroughly brought about this ownership of who they really were.

As the worship hour began, I felt more like a spectator than a participant. It was like a morality play unfolding, and it was a first in this little country church. One of the old women of the church, a pillar for two generations, came down the aisle as she did every Sunday. But this time, holding her hand was a little black grandchild. The service went as usual. No one even so much as cast a curious glance her way. Everything seemed to hang, as if it were suspended in time. Everybody went through the same familiar motions, down to the closing hymn and benediction, but it seemed that they were much slower motions. Something very large was happening to every person in the building. None escaped being drawn into a dynamic larger than their individual take on things.

After the service, a few of the men stood in the church yard enjoying a smoke. One of them was vocal, attempting to process what had just transpired. I caught the tail-end of the conversation when I walked up. He had finished with the remark, "We're bringing a scandal into the church!" There followed a dead silence. Then one of the other men took a final puff, dropped his cigarette and rubbed it out in the dirt and said, "I don't know, Tom! Jesus wouldn't have seen it that way."

Jesus would have all who follow Him and all who reject Him to look at their world through His eyes, to see themselves through the power of His super-vision. Having done so, they are free to go with Him or to remain behind, but they are never free to forget. Once they see life clearly, all that they behold becomes an irrefutable part of their experience. It cannot be left beside the road. It cannot become lost in the crowd. It must be carried and owned like a burden until, somewhere down the road, they encounter Him and are transformed by his love.

ACCEPTABLE RISKS
Luke 11:53-54

As he went away from there, the scribes and the Pharisees began to press him hard, and to provoke him to speak of many things, lying in wait for him, to catch at something he might say. (Luke 11:53-54)

There is a fellow I meet out on the road in the dark every morning. We pass at least twice each time, his exercise route always taking him in a different direction from my own. His demeanor has never varied. He focuses straight ahead, always passing me on the opposite side of the road from where I am. His concentration is total. He is passionately committed to a rigorous discipline and will allow nothing to interrupt it. Though we meet each other twice a day at such an early hour, he has never spoken to me.

On the other hand, I have attempted to speak to him. The first time I saw him, I said, "How's it going?" as he passed. He ignored me, but I know that he heard me. The next time, I just said, "Hi!" Still, there was no response. After a few weeks of offering a brief greeting and being ignored, I simply went my way as he went his. I stopped saying anything. And then, after a time of that, I was almost irritated to see him approach. I did not want to contend with his presence. In fact, eventually, ever so slightly, a little part of me dreaded going out, knowing that I had to endure the snubbing of a fellow-traveler.

At some point, I thought about how ridiculous my reaction was and how I had allowed this person whom I did not even know to affect my attitude and my behavior and set an improper tone for most of the days in my week. So I started speaking to him again. "Hi!" "Hello!" "How are you doing!" And I felt better about it. He hasn't spoken to me yet! He has not deviated. He is still out there with all that intentionality about his regimen, but he doesn't control my behavior or my day anymore. The world has a lot of iron resolve in it. It can be disquieting and intimidating. So much of it can even be defeating to the accommodating spirit when it must be confronted in its relentlessness day after day. How amazing it is that the game one plays in his head with some people becomes such an accurate read on life in the world. How literally amazing it is when every preservation instinct one has about the nature of a prospective relationship proves justifiable in a matter of time. The world is such that it is no longer affordable for anyone to be naive.

Those on the spiritual journey would do well to contemplate the risks and the hazards of the road. While everyone on it presumably is finding the way to the presence of God, not all agendas agree. Not all travelers are compatible. There are those on the road who make the journey a hardship for others. Perhaps they have no clue that they are doing so, but such is the consequence of their meeting and passing. The risks of this road are no less formidable than any other. Taking them into consideration, however, one has to determine whether or not they are acceptable risks.

Jesus walked many roads in His ministry. They took Him to villages and towns, to city streets and remote areas, to mountainsides and lake shores. He was always going from one place to another. So many times His life connected with others, and they were changed. But there were times in His travels when He bore the brunt of accusation and condemnation from those who, in their own set of different dynamics, were also on their way to the presence of God. These had the will and the resolve to derail not only His attitude and His behavior but to destroy His ministry. Their power was considerable, but they did not succeed. For Jesus, they constituted an acceptable risk.

One of the remarkable gifts of Jesus was His capacity to recognize the great cyclic behavior patterns of human beings. He knew about the tendency buried in the human psyche that would first greet and applaud and then suddenly turn upon the object of its interest. In a matter of time, the tendency would shift to one of denial and betrayal and crucifixion. It was an age-old pattern from which no person had ever fully escaped. Jesus recognized it instantly and, such was His wisdom and His cunning, that He placed himself in the center of it and became its archetype. His discernment and His courage in doing so have enabled countless human beings to follow, even when the road is dangerous. Because of Him, those dangers do not deter. They become acceptable risks.

A salesman whose product actually was dynamite did a lot of business with farmers and miners. His customers always needed explosives to clear their land. He had covered the same area for many years and knew his customers on a first name basis. But one day, he met a new customer who had just bought a farm and needed some dynamite to clear some stumps from the field. The new customer asked if he could be billed for the explosives.

The salesman asked him, "Have you ever used dynamite before?" The reply was, "Well, no! I haven't!" And the salesman said, "Then I'm afraid I'll have to ask for cash in advance." (Hodgin, p. 310).

Those who would follow Christ on into the presence of God must be acquainted with the risks involved. There are some which are so formidable that they deter many who would take this journey. But if one follows closely in the steps of Christ, even in the shadow of the cross, the risks become acceptable. One of the risks is **being misunderstood.** And to counter that risk, one must have an understanding heart.

The Scribes and Pharisees had no idea as to who Jesus really was. Trapped in their legalism, they defied Him openly and attempted to draw Him into arguments which they felt they could win. Jesus never avoided them, but He never fell into their verbal traps. He understood that they were confused about their own relationship with God, and even though they posed a threat to Him, He still dealt with them compassionately, with an understanding heart.

Inactive members give a lot of reasons why they do not come to church. I visited one who had not darkened the door in over fifteen years. As he poured out his story, he told me that he had offered to donate all of the labor and the lumber to build a recreational hall for their church and one man, who was a leader in the church, had thwarted the project out of jealousy. I asked the question, "Where is this person now?" And I got the answer, "Oh, he's been dead ten years!" I thought to myself, "How incredible!" And I said to him, "I don't believe I'd let a dead man keep me from coming to church." This inactive member eventually came back and was faithful and useful the rest of his life.

The risks of the spiritual road are not acceptable without an understanding heart. With an understanding heart, we are not deterred from our mission or detoured from our journey by those who would throw emotional and spiritual stones in our road. Though Jesus had those who hated and despised His ministry, He was not deterred from carrying it out. He calculated the risk involved. He was not naive. He knew what it would cost Him. For Jesus, it was an acceptable risk.

Those who venture out in their faith on the road to the Kingdom of God often do so without taking into consideration the hazards of the road. Others walking it with agendas of their own can pose a serious threat. If they are more resolved, more determined, more intentional, then they have the power to deter those who follow in the steps of Christ. One of the risks of the road is being misunderstood. Another is **being misrepresented.** To counter that risk, one must always represent the Christ of the road.

Thinking about how He handled Himself in the face of the many misrepresentations He received from the religious authorities, one is heartened by the style and the finesse and the engaging personality of Jesus. He never failed to represent Himself as distinct from those who would wreck His reputation and His witness. They accused Him of eating with sinners, of breaking the law, of blasphemy, yet they did not intimidate Him. Jesus clearly saw their behavior for what it was, and He pronounced it to their faces plainly in His series of "Woes" to the Pharisees and Scribes. In doing so, He exercised his confidence in His own authority and revealed their discomfort with their own.

Oscar Wilde once said that his Aunt Jane died of mortification when no one attended her grand ball. But she died without knowing that she had failed to mail the invitations. It is one thing to be misrepresented, but it is quite another to participate in the misrepresentation. Those on the journey, who follow in the steps of Christ, are always subject to detraction and nay-saying. It can wound and devastate and discourage, but it can never do irreparable spiritual damage if one will exercise confidence in the authority of Christ and represent Him in spite of the consequences. No one relishes being misrepresented or maligned, but on the spiritual journey, it is an acceptable risk.

The pianist did not come one morning to play for the service. It was highly unusual, for she was a fixture in the church. Faithful and dependable every time the doors opened, she had only one notable flaw. Every other note she hit on the piano was the lost chord. That particular Sunday, one of the visitors was a musician, college trained. Upon invitation by the pastor, she was asked to play, and such melodious notes had not been heard in that church for a long time. People enjoyed her soft, smooth touch of the keys.

Halfway through the first hymn, the regular pianist arrived and stood at the door, taking in what was happening. She immediately went to the piano during the course of the hymn and sat down on the stool beside the college trained lady and butted her off one end of the stool. The graceful woman fell in the floor. She rose, humiliated, and left the church.

The world is filled with obstacles and adversaries of every type. Some of them humiliate and bewilder. Some of them derail all the excitement and enthusiasm one has for the journey. While the world would threaten to undo even the most hearty resolve, all that is necessary to continue on the spiritual road is to follow in the steps of Christ. So what if there are concerns! They are manageable! So what if there are risks! They are acceptable! Nothing will detain or deter those on the way to the presence of God if their confidence and resolve and authority are greater than the sum of all that is set against them.

Nothing deterred Jesus! He handled all of the slights and the charges with an astounding grace, with a great gentleness. Even when He was betrayed and arrested and whipped and mocked, He was not diminished in any respect. In fact, these trials seemed to enhance His presence and power to those who were bent on eradicating them. Nothing they could do to Him, even putting him to death, lessened who He was. All they did to Him enhanced who He was. Though He did not want to die, for all that it represented at that pivotal point in human history, dying became an acceptable risk.

For those who follow Christ down the spiritual road, there are little deaths, little crucifixions which cause a tragic sense of loss and which bring their pain and grief. Yet if the culmination of these negative blows opens one to greater empowerment by God's spirit, the harm and the abuse and the mistreatment that are received become the means by which the journey accelerates and the witness is energized. For those serious enough to brave the dangers of the road, knowing full well how threatening they can become, **being mistreated** is an acceptable risk. And to counter the devastations associated with that risk, one must treat others kindly.

Remember how Jesus countered all of the mistreatment He received! "Father, forgive them!" He prayed for those who cursed Him, who abused Him, who destroyed His body. His prayers interceded for them before God. He prayed for them God's kindness! And, without their consent or cooperation, He transformed their minds and hearts forever. They could curse Him and hate Him and resent Him in their hearts, but they could never erase what He did for them.

For those who follow, for those who are committed to go down this road, every risk must become acceptable because every risk is what makes them fit for the kingdom they would find. Every risk opens the channel wider for the power of God's spirit to flow through them and work its will in the frailty of human flesh. Every risk is an opportunity to proceed more confidently in the steps of Christ.

A new preacher moved in after the one who had been run off. One family was chiefly responsible for the transition. The arriving preacher had been told he was going into a difficult situation, so he was wary. He tried not to repeat any of the mistakes of his predecessor. He did his best to be a good pastor, especially to this irate family, but he never won the family over. In fact, they seemed to have it in for him also.

He was there when they lost an elderly member of the family. He even did the funeral. He was there when their youngest son got his stomach pumped at the hospital from a drug overdose. The family grudgingly allowed him to fulfill his duties, but still he made no headway. The more he tried to do out of kindness and attentiveness to them, the more they criticized him.

When his tenure was up and it was time for him to move, he was packing boxes on a U-Haul when these people who had given him the most grief drove up in the yard. The man said, "When you get everything loaded, we want you and your wife to spend the night with us." It was a night to remember. It was a night of reconciliation for much of the anger and the sorrow and the betrayals of many years. Only the long-suffering of a pastor who never wavered in his kindness enabled it to happen.

The journey of faith is not without risks. One of them is cruelty and mistreatment by those whose very efforts have the power to crush the resolve and break the spirit. In the face of such formidable dissuasions, the one great encouragement is that Christ is the guide and one will not face anything that He has not already met and overcome. Because every risk was acceptable to Him, those coming along behind are undergirded by His amazing resolve, His wonderful confidence, His gracious authority. And He has assured them, "Let not your hearts be troubled! Be not afraid! I am with you always!"

Sources:
Michael Hodgin. *1001 Humorous Illustrations. Zondervan Publishing House. Grand Rapids, MI. 1994.* p. 310.

FORCED MARCH
Luke 9:23

And he said to all, "If anyone would come after me, let him deny himself and take up his cross and follow me." (Luke 9:23)

One of the most publicized episodes of World War II was the Bataan Death March. Following the April, 1942, surrender of the American and Filipino forces to Japan in the Philippines, this skeleton army was marched most of the ninety mile distance to the concentration camp. More died on the march than on the battlefield. Heat exhaustion, starvation, and dysentery accounted for part of the casualties. Others were the result of injuries sustained on the road from their brutal Japanese captors.

The Bataan Death March horrified and shocked the American people as have few other atrocities of war. Seven to ten thousand human beings died in a matter of days, their bodies littering both sides of the road for ninety blistering miles. Many of the soldiers were given no respite and were denied food and medical attention. At random, some were allowed to ride in trucks and were treated courteously while their companions, a half-mile behind them, were beaten and abused and murdered. *(f. Toland, p. 366f).*

We shudder to think about such things, denouncing them as cruel and terrible and unusually inhumane, yet such meaningless sufferings are not limited to war. People are mistreated, injured, and killed by one another every day. Illness and disease due to human neglect take a staggering toll, leaving behind as many victims as they spirit off. Life is no more tenable than it has ever been. It is still fragile and perilous and unreliable, and, at any moment, a casualty can be created from what was, only minutes before, a perfectly normal, healthy individual who never would have dreamed it could happen to her or to him.

Humanity is on the march, and the conditions are such that no one has a choice in the matter. It is a forced march which begins at birth and which gives no respite. Some fare better than others, but all are marching in this panoramic exodus of people and events, to their deaths, and there is absolutely nothing any of them can do about it.

Death is the one reality which is accepted in the conscious mind but which is totally rejected in the pit of one's being. That such an atrocity can and will be perpetrated against one's familiar and likable self is literally an unmanageable piece of information. Why should anyone have to die? More to the point, why should it have to happen to "me?" Such thoughts produce a paralysis and can profoundly disturb one's equilibrium, not to mention one's sleep.

No matter how logically death can be explained or how neatly it can be rationalized away as something not to worry about, the vast majority of human beings are terribly ill-prepared for it. They dread the thought of dying and are thoroughly frightened by death. They are desperate for a solution to this unthinkable and inescapable fact about their person, yet nothing given them has proven to be satisfactory. They continue to dread and tremble and sorrow and mourn.

Christian responses to death and dying have produced a fruit-basket turnover of attitudes which have done more to deny the seriousness of the charges rather than confess them. Death has been called a "friend!" People who are dead are described as "at rest" or "in heaven" or "better off" because they are dead. If explanations of this type are acceptable and, in fact, believed and affirmed by those who give them, why do they elicit the opposite emotional response?

Somewhere in the depths of human personality, the anxiety about death wreaks havoc with all the responses and explanations. The emotions riot, and no logical forces can bring them under control. What is needed is not an answer but a posture with which to cope with this precious but lemming-like existence. When one begins to look upon himself, not as a resident, but as a passing guest or a visitor to these parts, one does not have to concern himself with the matter of tenure. A tremendous relief can flood the being when one can admit he has no real stake in earthly life but is simply a tenant in a material structure who can, at any time, vacate it as naturally as he entered it and be on his way. Such a perspective is in character with the spiritual journey for it assumes that any dwelling place one inhabits is, at best, temporary.

Ministers and their families get to live in a lot of different houses. Some are larger than others, some older, some furnished practically, some lavish in their furnishings. Each serves the purpose and has that singular personality about it that most houses do. Families who have made their home in many different houses never think of always being at home in a particular one. Home is where they happen to live at the time, and home will eventually be somewhere else.

For the Christian, life in the body must be seen in those terms. The body is a temporary residence, but in time, death issues its summons and bids one elsewhere, and the dwelling must be vacated. To become enamored of the body is an expression of a materialistic culture whose values negate one's personal pilgrimage and the journey itself.

Many people who cannot bear the thought of their bodies deteriorating in a hole in the ground are assuming that death destroys the person in the body along with the body. That is a common notion that crops up in conversations people have about where "they" want to be buried. Requests like, "Put me next to your mother," and other similar statements suggest that the grave is the permanent repository for the person as well as the body, but nothing is more repugnant to a follower of Jesus Christ.

It is time to expose some myths regarding the event of death and to address some realities about it which fortify and justify Christian experience. Since it will happen, at some point, to every person, there is good reason to clarify some of the confusion about it and to identify those characteristics of it which relate specifically to one's faith. It is unfortunate that most personal reflection on the subject focuses specifically on one's doubts.

Something happened in the year 1752 that was peculiar; on the days of September 3rd through the 13th, nothing, absolutely nothing, happened. Those eleven days never occurred in Great Britain or in the American Colonies and nobody lived or died during them. That was the month that the Julian Calendar was discarded in favor of the more accurate Gregorian calendar, and the change-over required the loss of those particular eleven days of time. People went to bed on the night of September 2nd and awoke the following morning on September 14th. The days in-between never existed. *(Eckert, p. 226).*

The absolutely worst thought regarding death is that when it happens, one no longer exists, one ceases to be, life is over, forever, and with that, the thought of never ever regaining consciousness can be overwhelming in its emptiness. That possibility haunts more people than any other fear or worry they associate with death. That possibility explains why many Christians turn up in church on Easter but can't really celebrate the day. It is a possibility derived from doubt and not from faith.

A Sunday School teacher asked a little girl in her class, "What happens when you die?" And the little girl said, "Nothing happens!" For those who have thought it through and are without assurance and are inclined to agree with such a statement, let me assure you that something does happen!

On the spiritual journey, birth and death comprise all of the busy activity one finds in a large airport terminal. Flights are arriving and departing, schedules are monitored and adjusted, passengers are preoccupied with travel plans or are awaiting a change in conditions. Getting somewhere is uppermost in everyone's mind. Lives are in transit. Trips are being taken. Things are happening.

Responses to death vary with every faith experience, ranging from reactions of hysteria to expressions of somber dignity. Though all of them are acceptable responses, rarely are any of them affirmations. The occasion of death should evoke affirmative images for everyone traveling through this life who is associated with Jesus Christ. When death occurs, the journey is accelerated. **To die is not to exit but to enter!**

Death constitutes that passage from the material to the spiritual dimension. It is not so much an exit from one scene as it is an entry into another type of life. It is a total conversion from physical limitation to spiritual possibility. One should no more dread it than one should dread maturity. On the way to the presence of God, the event of death accelerates the spiritual journey.

My college classmates and I were shocked to learn that one of our favorite professors had been diagnosed as having terminal cancer and would be leaving the school. We did not know how to respond on that final morning when he met his class to bid us farewell. I entered his office after the dismissal to express some awkward words of sorrow and condolence, but he never allowed them to come out.

He raised a bony finger at me and a smile flashed on his gaunt face and he said, "Don't feel sorry for me. I have lived to do everything in life that I've ever wanted to do. This is the one experience I have not had yet. I am rather looking forward to it. I am fascinated by it, really fascinated!"

Jesus constantly reminded His disciples that the way He was going led to a greater and fuller life. They were not to be troubled by the thought of His dying, for His death would enable Him to enter into the joy of His Father. To die is not to exit but to enter! And also, **to die is not to lose but to find.** Dying has become such a self-indulgent trip that the way most people do it is a disgrace to the Christ who would teach them how. Nothing kills the prospects of this venture any more than a funeral, complete with the soft music and the crying towels. Such overly-reverent antics deny that affirmation can and should be going on, and whatever curiosity there is for it is confined to how good a job they did on the body.

Jesus said, "Whoever loses his life for my sake will find it." He would have everyone cultivate an insatiable curiosity about this next great phase. He would have everyone believe that death, when related to faith in Him, is the guarantee of life in Him. He would have everyone seek with enthusiasm the presence of God beyond the outposts of earthly life. Death accelerates the spiritual journey. To die in faith is to be christened and commissioned anew.

There are affirmations at the center of the death experience which challenge every person to a faith response. One of them has to do with our preparation for a new kind of life; another attests to the exciting discoveries which await us in it; but the most important one has as its focal point the purpose behind this awesome transition. **To die is not to remain but to follow.**

On the spiritual journey, one must never stop and remain at a certain place or a certain level. One must always take the initiative. If one follows Christ, there is a cross to deal with, death to deal with, but death is not the end of the journey. Those who follow Christ must be willing to follow Him into the life that is to come, continuing in His fellowship and entrusting to Him all matters of destination.

Columbus discovered America quite by accident. He wasn't really looking for it. He was trying to find India and just happened upon America instead. In the margin of one of his reports, he mislabeled the discovery, calling it Asia. He was like many explorers of his day, over-eager and destination-conscious to the point of inviting error.

Whatever else the scare of death does to us, it certainly makes us destination-conscious. There is the usual concern over places —heaven or hell, the right hand or the left, darkness or light! Such neurotic contemplations relate specifically to our doubts, and the purpose of this majestic existence is reduced to our limited ability to interpret that which we cannot possibly know.

Jesus said, "If anyone comes after me, let him forget himself...and follow." Our confession of His Lordship is what affirms us in death and justifies the Christian experience. To be in His company is privilege enough, for it is He who will bring us, at length, to the end of the way.

Sources:

John Toland. The Rising Sun. v1. Random House. New York, NY. 1970. pp. 366-367.

Allen Eckert. Wilderness Empire. Bantam Books. New York, NY. 1985. p. 226.

THE BURNING HEART
Luke 24:32-33

They said to each other, "Did not our hearts burn within us while he talked to us on the road, while he opened to us the scriptures?" And they rose that same hour and returned to Jerusalem. (Luke 24:32-33)

      A man who had not been back to that part of Maine in a long while was driving the car, showing his father-in-law the places where he had grown up. They had stopped in the middle of a country road, and he was pointing out the old farm house and telling some of the things that happened there when he was a child. He talked about the neighbors and how good they were, and how everybody depended upon one another. He remarked how times had changed and that people simply did not have that kind of world to live in anymore.
      As they were talking with each other there in the middle of the road, another car pulled up from the opposite direction and stopped. A man asked them if they were lost. The one who was pointing out the landmarks said, "No, I used to live around here. I lived on that farm right over there." The inquirer said, "You must be one of the Wheeler boys!" And the reply was, "Yes, our neighbors were the Proctors!" The inquirer said, "I am one of the Proctors." There was a long silence, and finally, the one who had come back to look at the farm peered very intently into the other car and asked, "Charlie, is that you?"
      Both men switched off their car motors and sat in their vehicles, side by side, having a very intimate reunion. They were there for nearly an hour, catching up on each other's lives. It was

an amazing coincidence, but what was more amazing was that the world and the people in it had really not changed all that much. *(Wheeler).*

You never know who you are going to meet on the road. You can go to the other end of the country on a vacation or a trip and bump into someone that lives down the street from you. You can go to Europe and often find people from your same town standing in an airport terminal. It is amazing how small the world is, no matter how far and wide one travels. It is amazing who turns up in little corners of it to surprise their friends and to dispel this myth about the world being such a dangerous and a different place. We never know who is going to turn up on the roads we take and refresh our spirits and change forever our attitude and our point of view.

The same holds true for the spiritual journey. Most who walk that road walk it by themselves. Often they feel abandoned on such a road. What a wonderful surprise it is through a chance meeting or chance passing to discover a friend who happens to be going the same way. Sometimes when we walk the spiritual road, we are too intent on what we are doing. Sometimes we go along gazing down all the time, and we miss or fail to recognize others who walk it just a little way ahead or a little behind. But if we happen to notice them, and if we by chance engage them, we will be amazed at how much this recognition will change how we feel about the journey.

This is what happened to two disciples of Jesus as they were walking to the village of Emmaus following His crucifixion. It had been a trying time for them. Their world had proven to be a very dangerous and unfamiliar place, and they were putting some distance between themselves and Jerusalem. They were lost in their thoughts and conversation, discussing the events of the past few days very intently. They hardly noticed when another person joined them on their walk and listened to their conversation. He inquired about the subject of their discussion, and they poured out their story of Jesus and how He had been condemned and crucified. They also shared with him the news that some of the women had gone to His tomb and found it empty.

As they walked along, the stranger spoke to them the words of the scripture about how it was necessary for the Christ to suffer these things. They were drawn by his words, but it never occurred to them until later that he was someone with whom they were intimately familiar. When they came to the village, he appeared to be going farther, but they asked him to stay with them. After a meal and much more conversation, they realized that he was actually Jesus.

Christ is always on the road. We may not look for Him, but He eventually finds us. We may not always recognize Him, but sooner or later, through being in His presence, His identity will be revealed. When that happens, things can never be quite the same. We find they are not as bad or as dangerous or as lonely or as discouraging as they were before we recognized Him in our company. Life after that is filled with greater energy, enthusiasm, zeal and interest, and we discover some of the joy that awaits us on this journey to the presence of God.

The journey has its discouragements and its crucifixions. It was true for the first followers of Christ; it is also true for His followers today. But the journey also has its chance conversions —those coincidental and chance meetings which reaffirm and reconstitute one's life. These disciples on the road experienced a chance conversion, and it filled them with such resolve and power that they did not tarry long in the village of Emmaus. We are told that they rose that same hour and returned to Jerusalem. No longer bowed with fright or humiliation or failure, these were new and different men. No longer asking each other about the events of the past by saying, "Can you believe it?" But going forth and saying to all whom they met, "Believe on the name of the Lord Jesus Christ and be saved!" Their journey was never the same because they recognized the living Christ in their midst.

Listen to their words regarding their encounter with Him: "Did not our hearts burn within us while he talked to us on the road?" Such is the character of the spiritual journey. Regardless of where one has been, regardless of what one has professed about God and Christ, regardless of how one has practiced faith and witness in the past, the chance conversion happens on the road due to an encounter with the living Christ, and one is never the same again.

When Christ is recognized on the journey, those who are touched by His power become intentional, sometimes even driven, totally reconverted to His will and His way. Such an unexpected conversion spurs them on, and they will do and suffer many things in His name. Such a conversion experience is characterized by the burning heart which ignites the life to a greater sense of urgency. It cannot stop and recollect or reminisce; **it must continue.**

So many people who ordinarily exercise conventional faith are like people who drive on the wrong side of the road in another country. They want to conduct themselves and their travel out of habit rather than intention. They have no clear sense of purpose or consciousness about their destination.

When one recognizes Christ on the spiritual road and experiences a chance conversion, one is spurred on by His agenda and direction. Christ is not just on their minds; His mind is in them. They have made room for Him in their thinking and in their decisions, and His power is evident in their witness. Such a conversion makes the heart burn with urgency and excitement, and it must continue.

"They rose that same hour and went back to Jerusalem." Such was the urgency of those two who encountered the risen Lord that they could not wait. Though they were obviously tired and had hoped to spend the night; though they probably had some business there for which they came, all these matters would have to wait. They rose that same hour! Such a conversion experience cannot pause in self-examination. It must continue, and **it must tell others.**

Perhaps the greatest common theme regarding the news of Easter, when Christ was discovered to be real and alive and in their midst, was the urgency with which all of the disciples went to tell others. "Go and tell," was the theme of Easter for all those who followed Christ, and those two who were on their way to

Emmaus were no different. Part of the conversion experience which makes our hearts burn within us is this insatiable urge to go and tell.

I got up from the kitchen table and left a sandwich half-eaten. Someone was pounding on the door, as though it were an emergency. I rushed to the door to see a man who was covered in silver paint. He introduced himself and, with excitement in his voice, explained the reason for his visit. "I've been down the road here doing some work for the city. They hired me to paint the reflectors on a bunch of poles. I've been disabled for a long time. This is the first job I've had in over two years." I said, "That's good to know, but why did you stop by here?" And he told me. "Yours was the closest house. I had to tell somebody!"

Check out the obvious people in the obvious places who have the good news of Jesus Christ. Check out the majority of America's churches. Does one find within them the burning urgency of men and women to tell somebody? Their hearts may be good and kind and filled with love and respect for their Lord, but if they truly believe that Christ is alive and well, they will burn with the urgency of His life within them.

A chance conversion on the road: It may seem like a questionable thing, but the soul knows, the heart burns, the tongue is on fire, the being is ready, the body responds. There are some things that just cannot be delayed or put off, and one of them is the conversion that is characterized by the burning heart. It must continue, it must tell others, and, finally, **it must celebrate itself.**

There are some towns in America and the world over which are known for unique things. There is a certain flower or shrub that is planted on every corner or up and down the medians, and the town is known specifically for that. Others may have an unusual number of a certain kind of bird, like the purple martin, and the town may thus be known to a passerby for that. Whatever it is that a town emphasizes, it is usually their specialty, and they find a way to celebrate it from time to time.

In services where the gospel is "celebrated" through worship or the sacrament is "celebrated" at eleven o'clock, one usually finds things dead to the world. The word "celebrate" is so over-used and over-done that most of the events described by such a word are not celebrations at all. They are normally half-hearted attempts which fail to celebrate anything. Yet those whose hearts burn within them will always find a way to remember and keep covenant with the Lord's resurrection until He comes. Such is the nature of the chance conversion that happens on the road. "Did not our hearts burn within us while he talked to us on the road."

Two young men named Richmond Nolley and Urban Cooper were hired as storekeepers by John Lucas, who was a merchant in Sparta, Georgia. Not only did Lucas employ these boys, but he took an interest in their spiritual development. Because of his influence, they attended a campmeeting three miles south of the town in 1806. It was a momentous occasion. There were 127 tents pitched and twenty-seven preachers who daily held fourteen preaching services and nine exhortations. The attendance at such meetings was a staggering 4500, according to someone who kept a tally. One of the fruits of that event was that both Nolley and Cooper, who probably would never have attended without the urging of their employer, were powerfully converted. Such was the urgency of this touch upon their lives that neither could go back to minding the store. After that one night, they were never the same again. Both became Methodist circuit riders.

Those who recognize Christ on the spiritual road are compelled to respond to His life and power. Their hearts burn within them, and their witness must continue, it must tell others, and it must celebrate itself. Nothing can prevent them from rising that same hour and going forth with His mind and His life within them. They have recognized Christ on the road, and their lives and fortunes are forever changed.

Sources:

story of friend, Charlie Wheeler, d. 1996.

THE LAST MILEPOST
Luke 24:45-49

Then he opened their minds to understand the scriptures and said to them, "Thus it is written, that the Christ should suffer and on the third day rise from the dead, and that repentance and forgiveness of sins should be preached in his name to all nations, beginning from Jerusalem. You are my witnesses of these things. And behold, I send the promise of my Father upon you; but stay in the city, until you are clothed with power from on high." (Luke 24:45-49)

I have a friend who has restored a colonial home and has spent many years getting it as nearly back to the original as possible, as far as one's eye for detail goes. He and his family live there, however, so there are also all of the modern conveniences. In watching this restoration project over the years, I noticed that one of the things he had propped there in his yard looked at first like a huge stone. In reality, it was an old milestone which had been anchored somewhere on an early road. In the stone was carved a number which told how far it was from a certain spot by representing the fourth or fifth milestone on that road.

My friend remembered just where that stone had been situated prior to its removal which had come about due to a widening of the road. He remembered as a child passing that stone in a buggy and later in one of the early automobiles. He remembered how comforting it was to reach that place and know from seeing the stone how far he had come and how far he had to go to reach his destination, but he had this to say: "They are things of the past. No one needs them now. At the rate of speed people travel today, a mile is nothing."

So many of the things that defined the boundaries of days gone by are so antiquated now that they are viewed as mere curiosities. Technology has pushed us past so many barriers and taken us far beyond so many of the established limits. There have been great leaps made in practically every category of life, and those who are not leaping with them are being left behind. Some of us have had to hang on to our hats as we have been pushed past most of the old mileposts.

Technology is not the only initiative that would take us places. Jesus Christ would have us go places, too. If there is to be progress made on this journey we are taking to the presence of God, those who believe in Him and who love Him must be motivated to go with Him out to the last milepost. But who will actually do it? There is more resistance from the faithful than from those who have never believed. Why? It is because those who are comfortable within the familiarities of who they are in Jesus Christ have no incentives to change. It is a resistance that is closely akin to the one experienced by many older adults who will not sit down and learn how to use a computer. They have the knowledge and the skill and the expertise to master it in stride, but they resist because they are comfortable within the confines of what they already know, and this new thing exists outside those confines.

The spiritual journey is not marked by familiar mileposts which comfort those who take it. Neither does it remind them at increments where they are and how well they are doing. There are places on the journey which, in order to be gained, must be reached by those willing to blaze new trails as well as walk the old roads. This journey is sometimes characterized by the labor of one hacking his way through a jungle, bent on making a path where none has previously existed.

This had to be what it was like for those followers of Jesus who felt the yoke of His great commission upon their own shoulders. They were to go and take the news about Him to the ends of the earth, and they were to start as who they were from where they were. How bewildering that news must have been. He said to them, "You are to preach repentance and the forgiveness of sins in my name to all nations. You are my witnesses of these things." How bewildering it must have been, yet they went! And here sit the rest of His witnesses so many years down range from that first great commissioning, not only bewildered, but resistant.

When a small group of businessmen and their families got together for a meeting, the excitement was electrifying. After a time of prayer and soul-searching, they made the commitment to start a new church. Most belonged to main-line churches which they said were spiritually dead. One of them made the statement, "They are more into maintenance than into carrying out the mission of Christ." In time their combined effort and influence eventually secured a piece of property that materialized in a wonderful new facility. Meanwhile the ranks were growing in Sunday School classes, Bible studies, prayer groups. The group experiences were the focus of this budding congregation which "made-do" with numerous retired and volunteer persons handling the preaching.

Eventually, the time came to secure a full-time pastor. This was done, and, at the outset, it appeared that the future could not have been brighter for this mission-conscious congregation. All of it quickly changed, however, once the church had to come to terms with its institutional future. What began as a fresh and adventurous vision of faith eventually came to bear a remarkable resemblance to all of the other churches in the community. The initial vision to remain separate and distinct from the rest became clouded. The pioneering spirit dissipated. The congregation became resistant to its own commitment.

The call of Christ in every age is crystal clear. It is a call to follow, to go with Him as willing companions, as followers so responsive to Him that He calls them His friends. Bewildered, perhaps! Resistive, possibly! But with faith enough in Christ to venture to the last milepost and even further in order to do His marvelous bidding. "It isn't impossible," He had told those first ones. "You will be clothed with power from on high."

So many spiritual assets and strengths find their way to those who pledge to follow where Christ leads. But within the minds and hearts of all who would walk this road, there must also be the inner resolutions which make one available to receive that power. No one gets brained by a spiritual wand and becomes empowered. One must be resolved to become empowered, and the first resolution is to **throw off every weight.**

So much of the resistance of those who feel the call of Christ has to do with all that clings to them. They are held back because of what they cannot leave behind. The world of the material and the relational has them in its clutches, and they cannot go where they really want to go. The power may be there to take them places, but there is no inner resolve to throw off all the weights.

In Jules Verne's novel, *The Mysterious Island*, five men have escaped from a Civil War prison camp by hijacking a hot-air balloon. As they rise into the air, they realize that the wind is carrying them over the ocean. Watching the land disappear, they wonder how long the balloon will stay aloft. The hours pass. The surface of the ocean draws closer, and so the men decide to cast overboard everything they can find, for they have no way to heat the air in the balloon. They throw out shoes, overcoats, weapons —and suddenly, the balloon rises. But it is temporary. Soon they are once again dangerously close to the waves. Again, they begin to toss out whatever else is left, including their food. Better to be hungry and dry than to drown in the ocean.

Unfortunately, this, too, is only a temporary solution. Once again, the balloon falls lower and lower until it almost brushes the waves. One of them has an idea. They can tie the ropes that hold the passenger car and sit on the ropes. Then they can cut away the basket beneath them. And so they sever the last possession they have, the last safety. As it drops into the ocean, the balloon rises again. Before it descends for the final time, with nothing left to throw overboard, they spot land. The five jump into the water and swim to an island. They live because they are able to discern between what was necessary and what was not.

The necessities they once thought they could not live without are the very weights that almost cost them their lives. (Larson, IP, p. 113).

Those who undertook the great commission to go out into all the world left everything behind in order to be empowered and to carry the Christ's message out into their world. Likewise, those who would follow Him now into the presence of God must overcome their resistance and resolve to go outside the confines of every milepost that holds them fast to what they know. They must resolve to throw off every weight, and the second resolution that must be made is to **hold fast to that which is good.**

In letting go of anything and everything that impedes spiritual progress, one is apt to end up holding onto little. But one must never let go of the people who need one's help. One must never let go of the assets that it takes to help them. One must never let go of the precepts which nourish one's responsibilities for those who are helpless or lost or forsaken along the way. Those who follow Christ must also emulate His life. He went about doing good. If progress is to be made on this journey, those making it must also hold fast to that which is good.

A young man was heckled a lot by his classmates, both in school and later, when he went off to college. Everybody thought he was a prude, and, if practical jokes were to be played on someone, he usually was the butt of them. He would suffer a lot of social embarrassments on occasions where he never seemed to fit. There, too, he was usually an object of ridicule. That he carried a Bible in his book bag and had a narrow upbringing seemed to be of tremendous importance to those who got a lot of mileage out of berating him.

That young man, after suffering many hardships and after struggling with some severe limitations, became a Baptist preacher. In later years, he was called to come back to the church of his youth, having served very capably in many places. Picture him as he stood there, white-haired and eloquent, preaching the gospel to some of the very ones, now grandparents and great-grandparents, who had made his life so miserable as a youngster.

It wasn't a case of "what goes around comes around." It was a testimony to one who, despite tremendous obstacles, held fast to that which is good.

When those on the spiritual journey can hold on like that to all that is good, they are not only marked as followers of Christ, but they are available to be clothed in His power and are enabled to do the work that He does. The journey is not just for traveling; it is also for commissioning. Those who walk the road with Christ are commended to walk it as He does, throwing off every weight, holding fast to that which is good, and there is one more resolution that must be made. It is to **open the mind to understanding.**

In the commissioning of those followers who were to be His witnesses, Jesus opened their minds to the scriptures which pertained specifically to Him. He revealed to them how the scriptures had been fulfilled through His death and resurrection. And He charged them to go, not blindly, but with an understanding of what they were to do. And it dawned upon them, perhaps for the first time, that they could not simply follow His teachings. They also had to illustrate them and commend them to others.

What constitutes the opening of the mind to understanding? The answer to that is simple enough. It is either a new idea or a new way of looking at an old idea. Christ's so-called followers in the here and now appear destitute in that department. It is as though their minds and hearts are closed rather than open to an understanding about Him that is critical and that can change and forever alter the limitations of the old understanding.

A ten year old boy in a farmhouse stood in the kitchen and watched his mother's teakettle boiling on the stove. The white clouds of steam puzzled him. Where did it come from? Where would it go if there was no spout? He noticed that the water sometimes boiled so hard that the steam jiggled the kettle lid. What would happen if all that steam were bottled up with no way to escape? Would the whole kettle rise in the air?

At a later time, when his mother wasn't looking, he filled the old teapot with water, tied down the lid, and stuffed the spout so tightly that no steam could escape. Then he placed the teapot over the fire that was burning in the fireplace and waited to see what would happen. After about ten minutes, the water started to boil. As the pressure built, the kettle did not rise in the air like a balloon; it exploded. One piece broke a window. Another piece broke a mirror in the room. Another cut a deep gash in the boy's cheek. The hot water scalded him from head to toe.

That night he lay awake, pondering not his cut cheek or his burned face and arms, but the experiment with the teapot. He was amazed at just how powerful a little steam had been. Perhaps it could be made to do things, useful things. That's what the boy thought about as he lay there. A few years later, he left the farm to study machinery and to tinker with engines. Though he eventually studied more things than steam, it was the exploding teakettle which directed the rest of his life. His name was Henry Ford. (CC, 1996).

There is tremendous power in new ideas. There is amazing power in looking a new way at an old idea, but if either is to be experienced, the mind has to be opened to understand what it has never fully and completely fathomed. When the mind is opened to understanding, bewilderment ceases, resistance ceases, and there emerges a great and wonderful availability to become empowered and sent forth from the last familiar milepost.

How is Christ contemplated by those who sit week after week in sanctuaries and Sunday School classes? However it is, a growing number would confess that it is without empowerment, without a clear sense of mission, without any great expectation or any new idea. However it is, no one appears to be embarking on a journey of faith equipped with any great resolve to venture beyond the prescribed and shrinking limits of what has been known. It could be called the faith that never takes one places, and in this society, it is about as useful as a stone milepost.

Those who have responded to the call of ministry and those who have resisted are among persons who are poised to receive empowerment. Externally and internally connected to the current of a faith tradition preserved in the scriptures, they have almost an inseparable identification with it. Because of such linkage, who they are is not confined to the personal; it is expanded to the symbolic. Once the symbolic is engaged, they are clothed with the power from on high, and they are propelled beyond all personal and social and cultural restraints.

During my tenure as a chaplain in a clinical program, the question of having prayer with patients during the course of a visit arose in a group session. Many views were expressed. Some felt that a prayer should be offered only if the patient requested it. Others felt that prayer should be offered with or without the permission of the patient. One member of the group suggested that saying a prayer as part of a pat routine on a visit might be a way of avoiding dealing with patients at a personal level.

The group leader that day was a Jewish psychiatrist. He stunned everyone with his unique viewpoint. When all the discussion on the subject was exhausted, he volunteered this profound insight: "When I walk into a room," he said, "I like to think that I am the prayer."

So many people haven't a clue to the empowerment that is already upon them to undertake the great commission. For those who understand the scriptures that relate specifically to Jesus Christ, the directive is crystal clear. "You are my witnesses of these things." And the empowerment is there to do all that seems impossible. How is it, then, that one can surmise all of this in the mind and heart and lack the devotion and the resolve to go? How is it that one, time and again, deliberately elects to miss the great discoveries that await beyond the last milepost?

Sources:

Craig B. Larson. *Illustrations for Preaching and Teaching. Baker Books. Grand Rapids, MI. 1995.* pp. 113.
Christian Clippings. Wesley Chapel, FL. 1996.

THE FATHER'S GOOD PLEASURE
Luke 12:32

"Fear not, little flock, for it is your Father's good pleasure to give you the kingdom of God." (Luke 12:32)

Ever since she was old enough to remember, Alice got the same thing for her birthday every year. She got other things, of course, different things which were in keeping with her age each time. But accompanying whatever presents she received from her parents, always there would be a card which held a promise. And this is what it said: "This card is good for one free trip to Paris, all expenses paid, on your eighteenth birthday." Her father kept the card year after year and always added it to the pleasures of the day.

When Alice was a little girl, she would dream about that far-off present. She would pretend she was in Paris as she played. She would tell all of her friends in school about the promised trip. She got more mileage out of that card every year than she did from all of her other presents combined. It was all she talked about.

As she grew a little older, Alice read everything she could about the city. She even bought a travel guide, took courses in French in high school so she would be able to speak the language. As the time came closer and the gift took on realistic proportions, Alice knew more about France and its customs, dress, language and culture than most people her age who lived there.

It was a gift that had truly captured her imagination from her earliest memories, and she had built upon those memories year after year.

Finally, on the eve of her eighteenth birthday, she was packed and ready for the one great trip of her lifetime. She had memorized her itinerary. She knew every place she was going, every meal she would be eating, every event she would attend. There was no more mature passenger on the plane to France than Alice, all grown up and finally ready to enjoy a gift that was for eighteen years the centerpiece of every birthday. What she did not realize until a little later was that, though the trip to Paris was great, she had already been enjoying the pleasures of it for longer than she could remember.

You and I may never know anyone who would do such an unusual thing and give such an unusual gift. But this is exactly how God gives each of us the greatest gift we could ever receive. He gives us the trip of a lifetime, and it is promised to us as early as we can remember. As we grow, we have all sorts of strange notions and fantasies about it; we make it part of our play as children; it occupies our deepest and most tender thoughts as we grow. We are told about its promise in Sunday School, and, if we go to church, we hear about it the rest of our lives. We can take the trip at any time, but most of us would rather just stay where we are and think about it and talk about it than go. However, it is ours, and it is free, and we can take it at any time. It is the trip that is identified as the Kingdom of God.

The Kingdom of God is like going on a journey. It is best characterized in all of the anticipation and the excitement and the preparation of a person about to take a trip. It is a trip especially designed for those who would follow Christ on into the presence of God. From the beginning, we are taught to seek it first, above all else, and the spiritual journey is commended to us, not as a way of reaching this kingdom but as a way of participating in it as we go along. Not everybody gets the promise of a trip on his eighteenth birthday, but you and I have been promised this one as a gift since the day we were born. "It is the Father's good pleasure," said Jesus, "to give you the Kingdom of God."

Can you imagine what that could come to mean if such a gift were ever accepted and enjoyed? It is the wish of God that every human being seek Him in this life, for by seeking, one prepares to live in God's kingdom. It is not to be a random experience. Christ is the companion and the guide, and He is up ahead on that road. All one has to do is follow where Christ leads. The best part of the gift has to do with the experiences that take place on the journey, for they are truly the experiences of a lifetime. They shape one's life and being, they direct one's future and destiny, and they bring one at last to God's presence.

For the better part of a century, millions of youngsters have enjoyed scouting. There are two things about the program which have been the most beneficial. One is the earning of merit badges, where the scout demonstrates knowledge or skill and earns a badge. The other is camping trips and field trips and hikes where one learns from experience and enjoys the many fascinating pleasures of a journey. While the badges are earned by a few, the trips are enjoyed by everyone, and no one has to earn or pay his way in order to go.

So many people who think they are on the spiritual journey have a very narrow understanding of the Kingdom of God. They believe that they have to earn the kingdom. They work for it. They do all sorts of things to be entitled to it. They can't get it through their heads that it will never be theirs through their effort. It is a gift from God that can never be earned, only bestowed. "It is the Father's good pleasure to give you the Kingdom of God." No one has to work for it. It is free to anyone who wishes to come along. There is no price for which it can be bought, no duty through which it is earned. It is free to all who desire to belong to it.

Have you ever thought about what people mean when they say "my church" or what you might mean if you say that? They aren't saying that they own it. It is theirs because they participate in its life. It cannot be theirs specifically because their participation is not exclusive, and yet their shared participation with others is not all there is to the equation. The church that they claim as theirs is much larger than the total of their knowledge about it, but even the parts of it forever outside their knowledge are theirs as well.

In one of the Sunday School hallways of the church where I serve, there is a wall which is a gallery of photographs of former preachers from a span of over a hundred years. Neither I nor the people who walk by these photographs each Sunday know most of these individuals, yet they are a part of our participation in the church. The congregations who heard these preachers and who were touched by their messages are literally unknown to us today, yet they are still part of this church. That part is so much larger than the portions of it I can identify and claim and know, so much larger than the current staff and congregation. It is ours, this church, yet the hidden parts that make it more than ours are ours as well.

The Kingdom of God is ours in the very same way. "It is the Father's good pleasure to give you the Kingdom of God." It already belongs to us, yet it is so much larger than all of the things we know it to be. Because it is, any talk of possessing it or having it is so finite and incremental that even our language cannot fit around it all. It is larger than the total of what we know, yet that greater and unknown portion of what it is belongs to us as well!

How does one take advantage of such a gift? How does one appropriate the Kingdom of God? If it cannot be earned by one's behavior or works, if it is a trip to God's presence, how do we discover it, and how do we process it, and how do we enjoy it? If it pleases God to give it to us, how may we be pleased in its belonging to us?

In all of his descriptions of the Kingdom, Jesus speaks in metaphors. They are difficult to apprehend, for they speak the language of the heart and not the head. We who would own the kingdom in our heads must first discover it with our hearts, and as we fathom the operations for bringing that about, perhaps we need to listen more intently to what Jesus says about it. One of the things He says about the kingdom is that **it is hidden from our eyes.**

He talked all the time about the spiritually blind who could not see anything yet who were quite religious. "They have eyes," He said, "and still they do not see." No wonder that many who are religious cannot see. The kingdom is hidden from their eyes, and yet, it is obvious in such a larger way. Jesus speaks about the grain of mustard seed which is invisible to the eye and yet grows into the greatest of shrubs, and the birds of the air make their nests in its branches. He speaks of the anonymous leaven which a woman hid in three measures of meal, and that ingredient did its work and leavened the entire lump. The hidden was really the obvious.

The Kingdom is like this seed and like this leaven. Its power is not visible, yet it is so large and so obvious. Those who would find it never do so in the world about them. It is a discovery, a spiritual journey, a way of apprehending the hidden reality which is larger than the reality we know. Those who would own this gift of the Kingdom of God must discover it with the eye of faith, for it is a kingdom which is hidden from the natural eye.

Another thing that Jesus says about the kingdom is that **it is valuable.** He cautioned those who were religious about spending their resources for things which were worthless and did not satisfy. And He told about a merchant who found one pearl of great price, and he sold all that he had to own the pearl. He told about a man who found a treasure in a field and who sold all that he had to buy the field so that he could own the treasure. Here again, it is the elusive which is really the most valuable, and one must sell all that one has in order to have the elusive which is of more enduring value.

The Kingdom is like this pearl and like this treasure in that to own it would cost one everything. But those who would have it are not able to borrow in order to gain it, nor are they able to retain their resources and their wealth and also possess it. It cannot be acquired by ordinary means. It is not like a commodity with a price tag. One is not free to have it until he gives all that he has for it. It is that valuable.

Another thing that Jesus says about the kingdom is that **it is primary.** It is more important than anything on earth, even one's own life. Jesus cautioned those who loved life more than the Kingdom. "Those who seek their lives will lose the life of the Kingdom, and those who give their lives for it will find the Kingdom." Of all the possessions one can have, the primary one is the Kingdom. It is of more importance than one's own life.

How, then, do we appropriate this gift from God that is ours from birth? How do we discover it, how do we process it, how do we enjoy it, how does it belong to us? It is hidden, but it is so obvious. It is free, but it costs everything. It is ours, but we must lose everything, even the life we know, in order to find it. You figure it out! It is perfectly nonsensical as an idea in our heads, but it is more perfectly accepted and cherished as a gift in our hearts.

The second thing about the church I serve is that it has acquired property for what may eventually spell relocation and a new facility. That is a provocative subject for many reasons. One of them is the breath-taking beauty of the present building which has served for the better part of a century, making it the only building of memory. Another is its down-town location in the heart of where most things happen as opposed to a fringe area of town where nothing will probably happen right away. While most are enthusiastic about the possibility of moving out and expanding, others have reservation and separation anxiety concerning what they know and love.

At the opposite end of the spectrum from the photo gallery of the old preachers hanging on the Sunday School wall is the infinite stream of new preachers who one day will hang there, and with them, all of the people who will belong who have not yet arrived. This stream, this sea of persons who will carry the church into the future lies beyond the limits of everything we know. We cannot comprehend it now and make it part of our knowledge now, for it is so much larger on this other end than a combination of the known and the unknown portions of what has been. All that has been is a mere step on the journey.

The largest part of the Kingdom of God is that portion of it which lies just ahead in the future. We are living out the pieces of one lifetime, but this kingdom is forever. It is not a place, as our narrow understanding would like to have it, but the pilgrimage of an unending lifetime. God gives us the journey of the spirit as the greatest possession of this life. Jesus calls it the Kingdom of God. It is the best metaphor Jesus uses. The journey is the essence of what God's kingdom is. But God gives it in such a way that Christ becomes our companion and friend, and we grow in the likeness of Christ as we arrive at last in the presence of God. That is how God gives it.

We dare not look for it as though it were to be discovered in the world about us. It directs every outward move there is, but it is truly not of this world. We do not find it by looking, only by going, and as we go, we will discover it, for it is the great and unclaimed possession of the heart.

COME UP HIGHER
Luke 14:7-11

Now he told a parable to those who were invited, when he marked how they chose the place of honor, saying, "When you are invited by any one to a marriage feast, do not sit in the place of honor, lest one more eminent than you be invited; he who invited you both will come and say to you, 'Give way to this man,' and then you will begin with shame to take the lowest place. But when you are invited, go and sit in the lowest place, so that when your host comes, he may say to you, 'Friend, come up higher'; then you will be honored in the presence of all who sit at the table with you. For everyone who exalts himself will be humbled, and he who humbles himself will be exalted. (Luke 14:7-11)

An instructor had trained his mountain-climbing team for twelve weeks. It had been demanding work. But considering the challenge that was ahead of them in a world-class competition, it seemed that all the long hours and all the long days were finally going to pay off. The team was ready. Each person on it was at peak performance. There had been grueling practice, night and day, in heat and wind and rain and snow —every possible condition that could be encountered in the actual event. The bulk of the hard work was over. The moment had arrived to pick the leader of the climbing team.

During most of the training exercises, the instructor had favored one over all the others, allowing him to lead most of the time. It was assumed by the group that he would be the natural choice since he had filled the slot on so many of the exercises. The young man stood there with that air about him that said, "I am the leader." He, too, was as confident as his team members, that he would be the one to lead. He had proven himself. He had the strength, the control, the experience, the overall best record. The plan for the climb had been his own. He made no attempt to mask his superior attitude, and had even maneuvered himself to take the lead position.

The instructor did a very startling thing. Without offering an explanation, he selected another young man to command the team. While he was not superior in all of the aspects of the other, who had dominated most of their training exercises, he was more group-conscious than any other member of the team. It was this group dynamic that would be needed if the team was to win against its competition. How stunned he was to learn that he had been selected, and how obviously crushed the other young man was that he had not. His shoulders slumped; he burned with anger; he felt humiliated and disgraced. For a few moments, his participation was in doubt, but, at last, he grudgingly placed himself somewhere down the line, crest-fallen, as though he had been handed the ultimate insult.

One can not always have first place or sit in the seat of honor. There comes a time when the proud are brought low; when the favored lose their status, when those who expect to be first must go to the back of the line. It is the way of things, and it is the way of the Kingdom for those who would seek it and who would ask to stand or sit in a certain place. This kind of consequence which registers at all levels from time to time, plays havoc with the idea of someone being special in the eyes of God. Oddly enough, this is how most believers conduct their spiritual affairs. They truly believe that somehow God has looked upon them a little differently, and that their uniqueness does not go unnoticed.

Jesus spoke to this attitude time and again in the scripture. On a number of occasions, He cautioned the spiritually confident about their behavior. He abhorred their self-righteousness, and He was all the time saying about such persons, "Truly, they have their reward." *(Matthew 6:2).* He implied that their ego was feeding their self-righteousness, and that had nothing to do with God. How right He was, yet how hard it was to convince His hearers of the truth of His sayings! Rather than hearing the truth, many rejected His teaching. And many who are in His Church today would do the same.

In churches and fellowships throughout the world there are people who sit in the highest place, in positions of authority, with leadership over others. Many of them are worthy. Many of them belong there. But even though they do, the Christ of the road would bid them to come up higher than their earned title or their bestowed status or their subtle but detectable self-righteousness. The invitation that is issued on the spiritual journey by Christ Himself is to come up higher, higher than the life we know.

All of us would be made more fit for the Kingdom of God if we would humble ourselves in this faith we share and take the lowest place. It is from this place that we are invited to come up higher, higher than the life we know. Humility is one of the sadly lacking virtues in our world, but it is a prerequisite for those who are on their way to the presence of God. God has greater things in store for us than those we would pick for ourselves.

It was during the Administrative Board meeting, and the chairman was new. The church needed a roof, and he was asking different persons to gain bids for the work. One older man who had a rather paternalistic history in the church said, "I'll take care of it!" The chairman asked him from whom he was going to gain a bid. He said again, "I told you I would take care of it!" The chairman explained that, while the offer was appreciated, it would be in the best interest of the church if all the bids made were a matter of record. The one making an offer chose to treat such a statement as a personal affront and turned to his wife and said, "Let's go!"

He did not darken the door for over a month. When he finally came back, he said a few words of apology to the preacher. The preacher echoed the regret and said, "We have all missed you and your family. By walking out and walking away, you have deprived us of fellowship and denied it to yourself."

All of us experience humbling moments. They happen despite our best efforts. One word wrongly spoken or wrongly taken can cause full-blown consequences. We dare not assume that heart and mind are in sync with Christ and that we are obediently following where He leads when one little word fells us. The Christ we would obey bids us to sit in the lowest place so He can tell us to come up higher, higher than an elevated sense of our own self-worth.

When we hear the call to come up higher, **it takes our eyes off lower things.** To be eager for Christ's approval, to be responsive to the worth that He would bestow, you and I must leave all of our unworthiness somewhere by the side of the road. Christ would have us see our own measurements by His standards, and He would have us give Him our full attention. No matter how worthy we appear in the imagination of our hearts, our feet are clay. Knowing that, we would do well to sit in the lowest place and feel at home there. Only when we accept it gladly and as the one we deserve will we ever hear the call to come up higher.

It was at a minister's retreat, and a few had gathered after the session and were in spirited conversation about difficult members. A few humorous stories were told, and then one remarked how he and his family had been deeply hurt by the jealousies and pettiness of one individual.

One of the preachers on the fringes of this conversation spoke up with startling information. He said, "These people you are talking about are who make us who we are. It is from them that we learn patience and kindness and humility from the flipside. They are the ones who put us in touch with God's peace, step by painful step. Later when we look back upon our lives, and we find that they are the real markers in our growth, we could go back and kiss them!"

The call to come up higher takes our eyes off lower things and enables us to see the divine shaping going on behind the scenes. If we keep our eyes on Christ and respond when He calls, we will see His winnowing in our conflicts, His grace in our trials, His ability to utilize us and those who grieve us for each other's spiritual growth. Christ would have us soar above the lesser lives for which we often settle.

When we hear the call to come up higher, it takes our eyes off lower things; and, secondly, **it takes our minds off ourselves.** One of the best ways to humble oneself is to consider the lives and destinies of others. If we practice that kind of humility, we lose our preoccupation with self and find a place in larger purposes. It can only do us good to concern ourselves with the desires and joys and griefs of others. It can only do us good to pray for them. It can only do us good to add our efforts to their struggles and be of glad and gracious help. Once our interests and concerns are trained on others, we are able to see ourselves in a more realistic perspective.

A priest who ran a food kitchen in a major city was inundated with a steady stream of persons, many of them reeking of alcohol, who wanted a handout rather than a hand up! He fed them, directed them to other agencies for clothing, patiently listened to their questions and their commentary. A group from another parish was there observing the operation of the kitchen, and one of the members of it said to the priest, "How can you spend so much time with such people?" He answered, "I want nothing back."

Let's not kid ourselves! We all want something from every conversation, every relationship, every human exchange. It may be a benevolent agenda, but it is an agenda, nevertheless. Yet every pause we make to give attention, to listen, to notice and to guide all those persons dissociated from the agenda may constitute the miracle which ultimately saves us from ourselves. In God's moment, we never know who is impacted for a lifetime from just such an exchange. It never happens when we are busy with our agendas which are generally rooted in the exaltation of self.

On the spiritual journey, the Christ we follow would encourage just the opposite. "Those who exalt themselves will be humbled," He said, "and those who humble themselves will be exalted." Christ commends to us the lower place, for it is from that place only that we hear the call to come up higher. When we do, it will take our eyes off lower things, it will take our minds off ourselves. And another thing it will do is **fix our hearts and minds on Christ.**

Christ seeks to accomplish His purposes in us and through us. One of those purposes is to bring us into the presence of God as we follow Him on the spiritual road. If we are to enter God's presence, we must do so in the same spirit as Christ. He would have us follow Him all the way there, but as we go, He would perfect in us the love of God. That love is not arrogant or rude. It is not selfish or boastful. It is kind and humble and good, and it is indistinguishable from the love of Christ.

In my home church, I remember the man who always sat in front of my family on the inside left of the pew that was the fourth down from the back on the right side. Every Sunday, I sat behind him and got to look at the back of his head. It was bald on the top with a ring of gray hair below the bald spot. I knew every hair on that man's head because I sat behind him week in and week out for years until I left home. He was always attentive to what was being said. He was always reverent. He was always present. He never knew I was back there, or if he did, he probably never thought about it. But his ever-present head in front of my face had an impact on a little boy who could always count on his being there. Every time I think of being in my home church, I can never visualize it without also visualizing the back of that man's head.

The interesting thing is that he never said anything to me that could be construed as having "directed my path." I never heard a word from him about his faith, yet he made the silent witness of his presence, time after time. Such consistent witnessing may make so lasting an impression upon a child that it will be modeled by tomorrow's adult if one's heart and mind are fixed on Christ.

Those who would make the most of this journey would do well to purge themselves of spiritual exaltations and agendas calculated to place them on the righteous path. "There is none of us righteous, no, not one!" *(Romans 3:10)*. There is none of us who is deserving to be praised for any reason. We all have feet of clay; we all have hearts of pride; we all have lives of sin and shame. There is no help for us in pulling up the boot-straps. Only when we fix our hearts and minds on Christ will He work His larger purposes within us and perfect in us the love of God.

    Always strive for the lowest place, for it is from that place that the Christ of the road will beckon, and we will hear the call to come up higher —higher than our self-righteousness, higher than our elevated sense of self-worth, higher than the pride in our deceitful and shameful hearts. He would teach us humility in all things, and He would place His love within us so that when we reach God's presence, our joy might be His!

GOING THE DISTANCE
John 13:36b

"Where I am going you cannot follow me now; but you shall follow me afterward." *(John 13:36b)*

Rosie Ruiz is the name of a young lady who was the first female to cross the finish line in a Boston Marathon some years ago. She was proclaimed a winner. Then the officials had second thoughts. Was it possible for Rosie to win? She had limited experience running marathons. Hundreds of photographs of the race were examined. Rosie was not found in any of them. So the decision was reversed. The crown was taken away from her. Instead of being a winner, she was a fraud, a phony. Although she crossed the finish line, she had not run the race. *(Meadors).*

Rosie Ruiz is typical of many who hope to gain honor and distinction without earning the right to it. Unwilling to invest the time, the labor and the sacrifice necessary to achieve worthy aims, they seek the shortcuts to desired objectives without giving themselves to the process. They want to be recognized a winner, but because the occasion is demanding, the discipline is rigid and the competition is tough, they do not want to go the distance.

Many Christians expect to finish their course in faith without having really given themselves to it. They expect to cross the finish line into the presence of God and to be applauded in the winner's circle when they have not fully participated in the spiritual journey or appreciated it for the necessary venture it is. While such fraudulent intentions may go unchallenged for a lifetime, eventually they are exposed, leaving those who bear them far short of the home stretch.

The journey to the presence of God is no small distance. One can travel all of life in that direction and still find that there is some distance to go. There is no assurance that those who die will automatically be propelled there, even though death accelerates the journey. There is only the assurance that those who follow Christ will be led there. Whatever a person's distance from God, such a person still has that distance to go.

Regardless of how much Bible one reads or how astute one becomes at the management of Christian virtues or how fervently one prays or how earnestly one believes, the journey has to be taken if it is ever to be completed. Religious gymnastics condition one for it, but they are preparatory exercises only. A commitment of one's total volition is required before the distance can be breached.

If one wades through a great classic of literature in order to say he has read it, or sits through a symphony in order to say she has heard it, the purpose of either has been wasted in the compulsion to finish what has not been fathomed. One can misuse the Christian life by seeking the end without fully discovering and being shaped by the means. Christian living should lend itself, not toward an obsession with its own end, but toward a savoring of the journey and of the values which are gained in its process.

Our society illustrates the danger of short-circuiting the sometimes painful process in order to achieve the instantaneous results. Children are victimized by crime and drugs and sexual experimentation because they resist discipline and self-denial in their rush to mature. Young couples are victimized by massive debts and high divorce rates in their rush to succeed and acquire. Older people are victimized by loneliness and alienation because, in their rush to reclaim what they never had time for, nobody finds time for them or takes interest in them. Ours is binge-living at its worst —fast food, fast cars and fast lives in a land where the American Dream ought to be like Instant Breakfast; no fuss, no mess, no preparation.

To deny oneself participation in the totality of an effort is to risk losing the quality of the experience. Only when one is committed from the start to the finish can he ever expect to discover the fuller purpose of the journey; and in that gradual discovery, who one becomes is undeniably determined by what one does.

The spiritual journey, like any other, begins with a single step, but it is not accomplished until every step is taken. No amount of righteous finesse will abbreviate it. No litany of pious routines will make it easier. Charles Colson, in his book, *Life Sentence*, put it this way: "The deeper one's commitment and the longer one struggles to follow Christ, the more distance one realizes there is to travel."

Some do not believe that it is a struggle to follow Christ. They believe it is a snap, and they would convince themselves and others that it is an effortless procedure, requiring simple obedience to a string of commandments which Jesus Himself reduced to two. All one has to do is love God and love his neighbor as himself. It might get a little sticky at some of the fine points such as turning the other cheek, giving the cloak also and going the extra mile; but, basically, it is uncomplicated and minimal in its requirements, with the only prerequisite being the faith of a little child.

Before one leans to that understanding, the fine points need to be investigated thoroughly. In His statements to His disciples about the suffering and death that awaited Him, Jesus realized that most of them were unaware of what was ahead for Him. They were zealous, eager, ready to follow Him into the fire, but He knew beforehand that they would doubt and deny and betray Him because they had many more miles to go in their journey. He said to one of them, "Where I am going, you cannot follow now, but you shall follow me afterward!" *(John 13:36b).*

Jesus knew that the great tests and trials of their faith lay down the road, following His resurrection. There were many steep paths ahead, many mired stretches through which to slog. To face the next few days with Him and die with Him would, by a short cut, eliminate some of the most necessary steps on the journey. It was not time for them to abandon the particular road they were on. There was still some distance to go.

The follower of Jesus Christ must be willing, not only to tread upon the high places where the way is glorious or easy, but also to trudge the lower roads. There will be times when the steps taken are tiring and painful, when the spirit balks or fizzles out in absolute refusal to go further. Indeed, there are days and nights ahead when the privilege will be counted as a duty, when one's willingness is challenged by one's resistance, when the command to follow seems pointless and is difficult to obey.

One cannot always follow Christ and do as one pleases. The journey to the presence of God is always dependent upon inner strengths, not just upon Christ's assistance. Those strengths for the disciples were discovered in His absence from them physically. Only when they were left behind after His ascension to contend with what they would do in His absence did they own and walk all of the necessary steps of the journey.

In his book called, *Positive Addiction,* William Glasser discusses his tactic for gaining the strength to do what must be done. In attempting to understand the motivation of long-distance runners, he concluded that these people were not capable of such a lonely, boring and painful commitment simply for the sake of exercise. He did not quite penetrate the phenomenon until he asked a runner, "What happens if you don't run?" And the runner replied, "I am so miserable that I really have no choice. I have to go out and run because I don't want the misery." *(Glasser, p. 42).*

Why do people follow Jesus Christ? Behind all of the perfectly sensible reasons, there is a similar bottom line; those who do would not want the misery which must accompany the choice not to! Yet in their desire to follow, there is always the tendency to become compulsive, to push themselves beyond what is reasonable, and to become impatient with that portion of the journey which is uniquely their own.

There comes a time on the spiritual journey when the progress made depends upon the initiative taken. To negotiate the difficulties encountered along the way, to bridle all of the irresistible urges and impulses which are part of its fascination, Christian initiatives must assume distinguishing features. What are the initiatives to be taken? What are the inner declarations to be made? One of the most obvious is **a patience with the journey.** Such patience is as much of a requirement for today's followers as it was for the disciples who followed Jesus, yet its acquisition is elusive for those concerned with spiritual progress and achievement.

The idea of moving from the staff of a large church to a three point circuit did not sound like progress to me. When I was asked to take that appointment, my first feelings were those of disappointment. I had hoped to have a station church with at least a slight increase in pay. As it turned out, I went to a rural area with a three hundred dollar reduction in salary and with a dismal outlook concerning the future.

When I voiced my disappointment to a friend, he said to me, "Look at it as an opportunity! You will have time there to write sermons, to enjoy people, to start a family. Trust the process! God is in this with you." While those words of encouragement did not inspire me at the time, how wonderfully right they were!

There is no limit to the efforts spent by some who are caught up in proving or improving themselves. They are zealous; they are eager; they are spiritually empowered and fortified. They want to do everything that is ahead with energy and with urgency. The one thing they do not wish to do is slow down, take the miles one at a time, or pause on the spiritual road. Instead of seeing virtue in patience, they view it as a waste of time.

Just as the disciples could not hitch a ride on Jesus' coattails but had to walk their own miles, the present day disciples must go that way themselves. The process may be incredibly slow, but there has to be a trust in and a reverence for the process. In order to go the full distance, there must be a patience with the journey, and there must be **a lending of oneself to it.** A second inner declaration is to have faith enough to forgo the immediate power to choose in order to be chosen in God's moment.

He was a capable preacher in mid-stream. We spoke in a parking lot about whether or not he should ask to move. "My peers have already propelled ahead of me, " he said. "I don't like to be competitive, but I am afraid that I am being bypassed and left behind." I reminded him of the great job he was doing where he was and how his time would come. "Worse than being bypassed," I said, "is to be propelled ahead and not be ready." The remainder of our conversation was spent with his sharing some of the truly great things happening in his life and in his church. I did not need to hear it half as much as he needed to say it.

There are those stretches of spiritual road where one encounters obstacles more internal than external, where one seeks bypasses and shortcuts to move beyond those times and occasions when the going seems painfully slow. It is then that Christian initiatives must assume distinguishing features. One of them is a patience with the journey; another is a lending of oneself to it, and a final one must be **a love for its shaping.** It is the shaping, not our own volitions, which make us equal to all spiritual opportunities.

He was in his eighties when I rode with him out into the county and down a dirt road for a few miles. We came to an old Baptist church which had closed but which still had a homecoming every year for the extended family who remained. His parents had married in this church; he had been nurtured by its Sunday School and baptized into its membership. He would be buried in its cemetery when the time came. It was important to him for me to see the place where he had been shaped and fitted for a worthy life. It was where he had embarked on the great spiritual adventure, and it was where this phase of it would end. What touched me more than his claim upon it was its claim upon him.

"Where I am going you cannot follow now. But you shall follow afterward." Jesus knew the importance of each person's developing the inner resources needed to make the spiritual journey complete. While His companionship is always offered, it does not impede or deny the gradual discovery of inner resources. While the ultimate destiny of human beings is with God, and while Christ is the companion and guide, there are places on the journey where one must find his own way. Progress may not be evident at first, but it manifests itself in the willingness with which each person makes the journey his own. It is from within this willingness that the journey is savored for what it is while it is, and it is every moment.

Sources:

Jack Meadors Jr. St. John's UMC bulletin, Anderson, SC. 5-11-1980.
Charles Colson. Life Sentence. Chosen Books. (Baker House). Ada, MI. 1991. p. 274
William Glasser. Positive Addiction. Harper-Collins. New York, NY. 1985. p. 42.

BEYOND THE BOUNDARIES
Matthew 5:3

"Blessed are the poor in spirit, for theirs is the kingdom of heaven."
(Matthew 5:3)

The great hymns of the church have always been a source of inspiration for the average Christian attending church in America. One can come into a sanctuary, feeling low and discouraged and unengaged by everything which is designed to lift one up, only to experience a sudden transformation brought on by some stirring piece of music. Perhaps the affirming words of a familiar hymn makes the difference, but, then, it may just be the power of the tune itself. Whatever triggers the response, there is personal engagement, motivation, and a surge of zeal and power through which one is personally connected.

This has been the impact of hymns, especially praise hymns, all the way back to the days when psalms were recited and sung on the way to the Jewish temple and up its steps. Some of these were denoted "songs of ascent" in the book of Psalms. While the meaning of that term is obscure, many believe that they were psalms written especially to achieve the motivation of the participants, to connect them at a higher level to the praise and adoration of God, to accelerate this process of transformation which is part of the function of the worship experience.

Sadly, many services of worship designed to connect and empower people fail and fall right off the edge of hopes and dreams and expectations. Hymns become dead recitations of the familiar. People drag through the creeds, doze through the sermons, and no one gets renewed. Worship becomes the weekly funeral service of the community, abstracted from the new life that spills over with wonder when one contemplates what it must be like in the presence of God.

Some things take people higher than they know, and one of them is this knowledge that all are on this journey to God's presence. Some of the forms that have been used to specify the journey may have become corroded because of time and care and a host of other factors, but the journey is as fresh and as promising as it was in the beginning. Regardless of what happens along the way in the form of discouragements, the desire to see God becomes intense and all-consuming. Though one realizes the value of the journey for its own sake, there is still this insatiable curiosity about what it will mean and how it will feel to belong in the presence of God.

People have asked in every age, "What is heaven like?" and they have concocted their own notions of it based upon what they have read in the Bible or what they have heard from others or what they have wished for themselves. In every answer that has been given, however, the preoccupation has been with one's worthiness or unworthiness, with how the self is perceived, not with belonging to God or with being as one with God.

While it is not for mortals to comprehend fully the meaning of everything they would like to know about God, even if it could be revealed to them somehow, the glimpses of spiritual insight that they do have are enough to convince them that there is more to be discovered beyond the boundaries of this existence than can be found within them. Entering the presence of God where all is energy and light, where everything accelerates, where spirits find linkage describes conditions for which most human beings are unprepared. There is a willingness to accept and participate, but there is an absence of skills and knowledge.

The combustion engine has proven to be a marvelous invention. Ever since the building of steam engines in the 1850s and the tinkering with gasoline engines at the turn of the twentieth century, it has advanced from a crude device to a marvelous product of technology. Along the path of its development, however, its limits have been determined. The space program in recent history has defined the critical ratio between the size of the engine and its fuel consumption as they impact upon speed and distance. Scientists realize that, if the universe is to be explored beyond our solar system, another kind of thought process has to take place which may have little to do with the combustion engine.

In this great quest of the human heart to arrive someday in the presence of God, one must begin to apprehend God a different way. God is not to be comprehended; God is to be engaged, met, belonged to! Beyond the boundaries of what one knows, one must trust explicitly in what Christ knows. Christ is the guide outside the parameters of what humanity knows and perceives of Him. What it knows and perceives of Him is on par with what is known and perceived about the combustion engine. There is more to Christ than the sum of everything known about Him, infinitely more. Apprehending that, humanity is compelled to follow Him, once it has owned the great demeaning of itself.

The bewildering thing about this journey to God's presence is that, the closer we get to thinking we are there, the further away we find we actually are. We are not purer in heart than we were as children. We have grown in our cynicism and our doubt and our fear almost as much as we have grown in our faith. We still cannot completely fathom what it really means to die. Our sins are exaggerated as we age, even though we strive to be good. Most of us who share the faith on this little terrestrial ball find ourselves reaching the same conclusion as Paul about our quest of the heart. He said, sometime near the end, "I am the chief of sinners." *(ITimothy 1:5).*

The enigma of this faith can only be deciphered from a metaphor. It came from the lips of Jesus in His pronouncements of what we call the Beatitudes. It is the first one: "Blessed are the poor in spirit, for theirs is the kingdom of heaven." This is no riddle. It is an explanation for why one's faith in God and Christ will ultimately fail. One's faith is littered with expectations. One can have every kind imaginable and rely on such faith, yet these expectations are what delude human beings and ultimately shatter their faith. It is in the shattering that one comes to know the great poverty of the spirit.

To realize one's utter helplessness and powerlessness and to know the absence of every expectation of faith is to know the impoverishment of the spirit. To become a spiritual pauper, destitute of the last vestige of spiritual entitlement, is to be made fit for the Kingdom of God. "Blessed are the poor in spirit, for theirs is the kingdom of heaven."

On the spiritual journey, the real transformation comes when our last, best fantasies about it are broken, when our presumptuous hopes are shattered, when our total apprehending of how things are is called into question. Then and only then, in the poverty of our spirits, are we ready to go beyond the boundaries and belong to the heart of God. If it is to happen, we must **say the hard good-byes.**

A poet said it this way. "We learn and we learn and we learn and we learn. With every goodbye, we learn." Friends moving away from a home they have known for thirty years, children leaving home for the first time, people kissing their dying relatives for the last time know what it means to say good-bye. But there are harder good-byes. They have to do with letting go of the self one knows and loves, the self with which one is thoroughly familiar, the one that has taken the journey and has prepared heart and mind and consciousness for the great event of God's presence. Saying good-bye to that self is the hard good-bye.

The woman who gives up much of her identity in the rearing of children; the child who stays at home to care for aging parents; the accident victim who wakes up a paraplegic knows what it means to say good-bye, but to say it to one's spiritual identity, to one's "special" relationship with God is to say a much harder good-bye.

It is difficult to define what it will be like beyond the boundaries of the highest thought and the greatest faith, but if one is to journey there and know the Christ one follows, if one is to belong fully to God who waits and who will receive, one must say the hard good-byes. Then one must **open the heart's windows.**

There are places in us which have never known the touch of light or love. They are secret places, not even we know them all. The ones we do have knowledge of, we sealed off long ago. In them are stored our greatest vulnerabilities, our tenderest affections, our inexpressible joy. We are afraid for anyone to know about these places. We even lie about them to ourselves, but after we have been reduced by the poverty of the spirit and every shred of defensiveness is removed, after the ego has been punctured and all control is relinquished, we can throw open the heart's windows and know for the first time the value of what is in these places.

From time to time, members of my congregations have owned and operated recreational vehicles. Some of them have taken a month or two in the summer to tour the country in them, traveling from the east to the west coast or visiting the Grand Canyon. The great majority, however, have not gone that far. They have settled for a week or two in Florida or just being hooked up on a cement pad in a state park.

For the lack of a better word, many of these people referred to themselves as campers, yet look at the degree to which they "rough it!" Some RV's cost more than a mobile home! Most are equipped with kitchen, bathroom, shower, septic tank. The view on the outside might be different, but the inside has all the comforts of home. In their adventures to new horizons, people I have known have taken with them most of the familiar conveniences and have never viewed it as somewhat contradictory.

The new life of the spirit which Christ would have all engage can be touched and tasted here, but because it must be experienced from the same old human frame of reference, it must carry with it many of the trappings of the old life. Perhaps the only way it can be truly and authentically engaged is for one to know the poverty of the spirit. The poor in spirit are those who have reached the point on the journey where they can say the hard good-byes, open the heart's windows, and **breathe in God's peace.**

Leaving the pressures of the work place and the responsibilities of home and family and going back to the home of one's childhood, if it is still there, is good therapy one or two days out of a year. Just to be back in an aura of acceptance where nothing is required, nothing overwhelms, nothing spells urgency is to breathe a sigh of relief. On the other end, to be right in the middle of one's purpose in life, to be at one with all the differences that are being made, to know that one is doing what one was born to do, becoming lost in its bliss and its flow are also to breathe a great sigh of relief.

There are signs all around us that give us inklings of what it must be like to breathe in God's peace. We never do it fully, however, unless we have known what it means to be one of the poor in spirit, who has been stripped of all spiritual possessions, and has been propelled toward a transformation which is total and eternal in the changes that it brings. While it is thorough and reconstituting and while it fits us to belong in the presence of God, the greatest of its liberations is its great sigh of relief over this world and this life. It is what must happen to each of us if we are to follow Christ beyond the boundaries.

In a popular piece of fiction of our time, persons are on a quest of the heart, attempting to fathom a number of spiritual insights revealed by ancient documents. One after another, they understand and master the teaching of each one. So ultimately transforming are these insights that they totally reconstitute the persons who are drawn to them and who begin to live by them. Toward the end of the book, in the apprehending of the last insight, the people who discover and implement it develop a capability to translate themselves physically, through practice, from fleshly form to spiritual energy. (Redfield).

While this sounds like pure fiction, it is where Christ would take everyone who follows Him on the spiritual journey —out of our poverty, into His riches; out of our selfishness and our loneliness into God's presence; out of our darkness and into His great light; out of this life and into the life to come.

Sources:

James Redfield. *The Celestine Prophecy.* Warner Books. New York, NY. 1994.